DESERTED LOYALTY

An Outlaw Biker Tale

Alex McRae

Published by Iron Battalion Press

Made in the USA

2025

Visit Alex McRae at www.alexmcrae.net to sign up to the author's newsletter and learn more about Iron Battalion books.

Twitter : @AlexMcRae99

Instagram: @alexmcrae99

Amazon : https://www.amazon.com/stores/Alex-McRae/author/B0F344WTHB

PROLOGUE

Southern California, the early 2000s. The town of San Carmelo is one of the largest counties in the USA.

Ryder and Vince, two outlaw bikers from the legendary Iron Ravens Motorcycle club, sat in Vince's battered El Camino watching the shabby nondescript building across the street. A steady flow of shady types was in and out of the building all morning.

"Okay, so what are we looking at here?" asked Ryder.

"You know what that building is," asked his lifelong brother Vince.

"Hmm, let me guess, off-track betting?" said Ryder.

"Not even close," smiled Vince 'Take another guess."

"Dude, I have no clue, just tell me," snapped Ryder.

"A dispensary!" Vince announced with a big shit eating grin.

"Um, ok. What are they dispensing with?" asked Ryder.

"Dude, cmon now! It's a legal weed joint." Vince explained.

'What? How can that be legal?" asked Ryder,

"Look, here's the deal. Anyone with a medical marijuana card can just walk in there and buy weed legally," said Vince.

"No way! That's crazy," said Ryder. "How can that be legal?"

"Well, here's where it gets interesting. Under California law, these places can sell weed."

"Yeah, you said that," Ryder added.

"No. Let me finish," said Vince, "Under California law, they can sell weed. However, there is no federal law about banking the profits of weed."

"Okay and ....?" asked Ryder.

"Sooo these dispensaries do thousands of dollars in transactions a day," said Vince. They can't use the banks to secure their cash."

"So what do they do with it?" asked Ryder.

"Well, some use local credit societies to do their banking," said Vince, "But many just stash it because they can't risk the Federal banks confiscating it."

"Ahh, I see," said Ryder.

"But do you really see?" asked Vince, "Places like this have more cash on hand than a bank and less security. We go in, wave our pistols about, grab the cash and get the hell out of there."

"It's that easy?" asked Ryder.

"Sure, I mean, I doubt if the cops will even care. Most cops can't stand the dispensaries even if it's now technically legal," said Vince. "More money and safer than robbing a bank, bro. Easy money. Trust me"

"So, what ya thinking?" asked Ryder.

"My guy says they do all their banking on Fridays, half goes to the local Credit bank, and the rest goes to the owner's house. We go in just before closing on Thursday night, and they will have a week's worth of cash on hand. We relieve them of it, and then we pack up and move to Arizona, bro."

"Really? We will have enough to start again?" asked Ryder.

"Yeah, man. We can move to Arizona and start our own motorcycle shop just like we always planned," Vince replied.

"Why not just start one here?" asked Ryder.

"Bro, local law enforcement knows us too well here. We both have convictions up the wahzoo. You think if all of a sudden we become 'cash rich', they are not going to put two and two together and realize it was us who robbed the weed place?"

'Ah yeah, you got a good point," said Ryder.

"We both made a lot of mistakes growing up in this shit hole town, bro. The way I see it, this job is our ticket to a fresh start. A chance to re-invent ourselves where no one knows us or our families."

"Yeah, I hear that," said Ryder. Both he and Vince had bonded over their crappy family lives. Well, that and their love of motorcycles. They had started on dirt bikes as kids, gotten into skateboarding in their teens, before returning to motorcycles in their late teens. 'So we're gonna move to Phoenix?

"Nah, nah, way too hot there, man. I am thinking of some small town in Northern Arizona, maybe near Flagstaff or somewhere." Vince replied.

Yeah, good thinking, bro," said Ryder 'So this Thursday night, yeah?"

'Here's what I think we should do," said Vince. 'We will park our cars behind that supermarket on Foothill Boulevard, but you steal us a getaway car. We drive up here. Rob the place, drive straight back here. Switch out to our own cars. Go home, grab our gear and get out of town."

'Okay, got it, what about disguises?" asked Ryder.

"I have us fresh pairs of coveralls and two ski masks. Oh yeah, hit up Payless and grab some low-budget sneakers tomorrow too."

"Why Payless?" asked Ryder

'First off, they're super cheap – we will need to ditch them when we change clothes," said Vince. "Secondly, they're very common. If we leave a shoe print, there will be a million schmucks wearing the same footwear."

'Ahh, smart," said Ryder. "Anything else?'

'I think that's it," said Vince. 'I'll call you later if I think of anything else that is important."

Vince put his El Camino in drive and pulled out of their parking spot across the road from the dispensary. He was confident this would be the one job that would set them up for life.

The pair met up at 4 pm that Thursday afternoon. The car park in front of the supermarket on Foothill was busy, but when Ryder pulled around back, it was relatively deserted. A couple of cars peppered here and there, but no customers. Probably only used by the staff, thought Ryder.

Vince pulled in moments later in his battered El Camino, parked and walked over to Ryder with a couple of sports bags.

"Here ya go, bro," he said, tossing Ryder a black ski mask and a set of mechanics coveralls.

"Thanks," said Ryder, catching the clothes in his left hand. He sat down in his car, pulled off his black leather engineer boots and pulled on the coveralls. He then pulled the ski mask over his head, but rolled it up to look like a woolen beanie.

As instructed, he had picked up a cheap pair of $20 Air Walk sneakers from Payless yesterday and put those on, too.

'You all good?" asked Vince.

'Yeah, brother, ready to rock and roll," Ryder replied. He could already feel the adrenaline coursing through his body. He felt good. He felt alive.

'What about a car?" asked Vince.

Ryder looked around. These cars were probably the employees, who were to say when they were to start or finish their shift? If he stole one of these and the owner came out while they were robbing the weed place, they would call the cops. The last thing he and Vince needed was to return to a car park full of cops.

"I don't see anything here worth taking," said Ryder 'Let me walk down the alley and see if there are some better options."

Okay, you do that," said Vince. "Hey, ya got your pistol right?"

'Of course, bro, I don't leave home without it," Ryder replied.

Vince returned 10 minutes later with a late-model Honda Accord. He recalled reading somewhere that it was one of the most popular stolen cars in the USA. He could see why. Took him seconds to jack.

'All set, bro?" asked Ryder, hanging out the window of the stolen Accord as he returned to the rear car park of the supermarket.

'Yeah, let me load up," said Vince, pulling open the back seat and tossing in their sports bags.

10 minutes later, they were sitting in front of the dispensary.

Ryder checked his watch, 630pm. According to Vince, this dispensary closed at 7 pm.

"6.30 bro. What time ya wanna do this? He asked.

Vince checked his own watch. "Hmm, 15 minutes, brother."

'Sounds good," Ryder noticed that Vince also had his ski mask on top of his head, like a beanie.

As they watched the dispensary in their rear view mirror, they saw a couple of customers leave the premises, jump in their car and drive away. Ryder scanned the car park; two other cars out front. *Were they customers' or staff cars?*

5 more minutes passed, and another customer exited the building, got in their car and left. Okay, so one more car to go.

'One car left," Vince announced.

"Yeah!" Ryder replied. He checked his watch again at 6.40 pm. 5 minutes.

It was now 6.45 pm. The one car was still there. Must be a staff member's car, Ryder figured.

"You ready, brother?" asked Ryder.

"Yeah, look, we got this. Easy job. When we leave, though, head North," said Vince

"North? The Supermarket is south of us, though," said Ryder.

"Yeah! Exactly. No doubt the cops will ask them, "Which direction did they go?" They will all say North, thinking we are heading to Berdoo or somewhere. Meanwhile, we take a side street, double back and head south to the supermarket."

'Ahh yeah, good thinking bro," said Ryder. 'Ok, time to make some money, be safe brother"

'You too," said Vince, exiting the stolen vehicle and reaching in and grabbing the sports bags. He tossed one over the hood of the Accord to Ryder and kept the other for himself.

The robbery went better than expected. As soon as they entered the premises, Vince let off his shotgun into the ceiling just to scare everyone. There were 3 staff on hand, zero customers and none of them were foolish enough to put up a fight. Vince had been correct on his intel, which was way, way easier than robbing a bank. They forced the staff into the back room and made the manager unlock the safe. There had to have been at least $500,000 in cash in there. As Ryder held his pistol on the 3 employees, Vince loaded the money into the two sports bags.

After a heart-stopping 90 seconds, he was ready. He slid one of the bags across the floor 'Are you ready, Kevin?" he asked.

Ryder realized he was using a bogus name to throw the scent off when these guys filed a police report.

'Yeah, I'm ready, Dean," Ryder replied.

'Let's get out of here then," said Vince. They stuffed the 3 employees into the manager's office, then shut the door, and Vince battered the lock with the butt of his shotgun. It wouldn't hold them off for long, but it should be enough time for them to make their escape.

They raced out to the waiting Honda and jumped in. Ryder spun the car around, and just as they planned, they headed North,

"Whooooo. That was amazing. Just as you said, bro," Ryder shouted, his heart going 100 miles an hour.

"Hey, hey, try and slow down a bit, bro, we don't want to get caught speeding," Vince replied.

"Yeah, good call," said Ryder, easing his foot off the gas. As he slowed down, he could hear sirens in the distance.

'Sirens? Already? WTF?" asked Ryder.

"Shit, I dunno man, maybe one of them had a cell phone or something? I ripped the land line out of the wall," said Vince. 'Quick turn here"

Vince pointed to a side street that would get them to another major road to head south on. Soon they would be back at the supermarket. Dump the stolen car, dump their gear and be on their way to start their new lives.

Ryder made the turn, headed two blocks west and then made another quick turn to run them back south again. He looked at the car's dashboard clock. By his estimates, they would be back at the supermarket in 7 minutes.

What bothered him was the fact that he could hear more police sirens in the distance. *Why on earth would the cops care about a bunch of hippies getting robbed?* Thought Ryder.

"Dude, try and hurry, sounds like more cars on our tail," Vince urged.

"Yeah, I'm doing my best," snapped Ryder, trying to go as fast as possible without attracting further attention.

After a few minutes of weaving in and out of traffic, Ryder could see the neon for their supermarket in the distance. They were almost there. He slowed down and tried to drive like he was just on a grocery run.

He reduced speed and cruised through the parking lot to the rear of the building. He pulled up next to Vince's El Camino.

He slung off his coveralls and mask and tossed them into the front seat of the Accord.

He tossed his sports bag filled with dollar bills into his car. Then he sat down, pulled off his sneakers and tossed them into the Accord too. He looked over to see that Vince was doing the same. He figured they would torch the little Honda and get out of there within 2 minutes.

Vince, now back in jeans and a flannel, approached Ryder from the passenger side of his car. In the distance, the sirens were getting louder and louder.

"Hey, man," said Vince from behind Ryder.

'Yes?" asked Ryder,

'I just wanna let you know. You're gonna be okay," said Vince

"Huh?" asked Ryder. *What was he talking about?*

He felt a slight sting in his lower back.

"Owww fuck! What was that?" he yelped. He turned to see that Vince had a small hypodermic in his hand.

"Sorry, bro," said Vince, looking genuinely sorry.

'Dude? What did you do? Vince, man, what did you do?" asked Ryder, starting to feel dizzy.

'Sorry, man"

Ryder struggled to remain conscious. The police sirens were almost deafening now. The last thing he remembered was Vince going through his sports bag before he passed out in the seat of his car.

CHAPTER 1

It had been 6 months since Joe "Moose," Murdock had gotten back from his disastrous trip to Mexico, where he had lost both his best friend Johnny "Ace," McIntire and old mentor Hank "Old Man," Carter. He was still haunted by dreams of Johnny speaking to him, many times waking in the middle of the night in a cold sweat. There was no one he could talk to and confide in about what happened on that run to Mexico, well, at least no one would understand what really happened.

Since returning from Mexico, Joe had decided to change his life. He had sold the home he had owned in the Phoenix Metro area and moved further north to the small upstate town of Pine Hollow. Set between Snowflake and Flagstaff, Arizona, Pine Hollow had all the benefits of small-town living but was close enough to Flagstaff if he needed to get back to "civilization," so to speak. After growing up in Tucson and then moving to Phoenix, it made a refreshing change having 4 seasons and cooler summers in Pine Hollow.

He had managed to score a job at a local bike shop run by a member of his former club, the Steel Reapers Motorcycle Club. The owner, a guy 20 years younger than Joe, was a cool dude named Clay. Clay wasn't the sharpest knife in the drawer, but he seemed well-liked by everyone in town and lived and breathed motorcycles.

Joe had been wrenching on bikes his whole life, so the work was easy, but he also found himself helping out with the shop's accounting, the ordering of parts and the buying and selling of used bikes. Truth was, probably 4 hours a day of his time was getting his hands dirty, and the rest was all the other stuff that went into running a bike shop in this day and age.

Since he had moved to Pine Hollow, he had gotten to know most of the locals, who were all super nice people. Many of them knew how special the town of Pine Hollow was and had no desire to venture into big cities like Los Angeles or New York City, except for maybe a vacation. Joe could respect people who valued what they had.

He was renting a small house 2 blocks off Main Street, so he could really walk to and from work every day. That said, at least three times a week, he would ride his Harley into town and go exploring after work. He loved losing himself in the tall pine forests that peppered the landscape between Pine Hollow and Flagstaff. Sometimes he felt like he was living in Colorado and not Arizona; it felt so surreal.

A few nights a week, he would go into the local dive bar, the Dead Crow Saloon and drink a couple of beers, not to get wasted but just to chill out and reflect on his life. Then he would walk home on the empty streets of small-town USA. It was a simple life, but after years of action and excitement, he was at the stage in his life where this felt right.

Today was going to be a special day. For the first time since opening the motorcycle shop on Main Street 6 months ago, Clay and his girlfriend Nina (who was one of the best bartenders at the Dead Crow) were heading out on a well-earned vacation to Rocky Point, Mexico (Puerto Penasco, aka Arizona's beach) and leaving

Joe in charge of the shop. It showed a huge leap of faith from Clay and the club to leave Joe in charge, and he was determined not to let anyone down.

Clay stood there going over the list of things he needed to take care of during his absence.

"So you all clear on what needs to be done then, Moose?" asked Clay.

"Yeah, buddy. Rebuild the engine on that Panhead. Swap out the handlebars on that Evo for some ape hangers and hard tail that frame on the Honda Shadow," Joe replied, "Am I forgetting anything?"

Clay thought for a moment, "Hmm, that about covers it, I think. Oh yeah! Try to sell that Sportster up front. Hmm, and of course accept any mechanical work that comes through the door when I am gone."

"Of course, boss," Joe replied.

"I'm going to leave you a number for the resort we will be staying at down in Rocky Point," said Clay

"Well, you can leave it, but unless World War 3 kicks off and the Russians invade Pine Hollow, I will try not to call you, alright?" Joe replied.

"Yeah, definitely call me if the Russians invade Pine Hollow Moose! Red Dawn was one of my favorite movies growing up," Clay laughed.

'Wolverines!" shouted Joe.

'Fuck yeah," Clay replied, "So, do you have any questions for me before I say goodbye?"

'Nah, I think I am good," Joe replied. "Have fun and try not to get too sunburnt. The sun hits harder down there for some reason."

"Thanks, buddy. I'll do my best," said Clay. "Alright, I gotta roll, want me to text ya when we get there?'

"Up to you, man, I have my work cut out for me here today. I probably won't even check my phone till after 6 pm."

"Ah, okay, I'll probably just drop ya a text anyway," said Clay

"Works for me, brother," said Joe.

Clay left, and Joe got on with the day's work. He was so engrossed in rebuilding the Panhead engine that when his phone finally did ping and he checked it, he was surprised to see that it was after 6 pm. It was Clay, letting him know that he and Nina had safely arrived at their resort in Rocky Point.

He sent a text back, "Cool," and got back to work. The truth was his cell phone had gotten him out of the "zone," and now he realized he hadn't eaten anything since breakfast. After 6 pm, his food options on a weekday in Pine Hollow were limited. So, he figured he would close up shop and hit the Dead Crow Saloon for a beer and a burger.

After shutting up shop, Joe walked the 4 blocks to his favorite bar, the Dead Crow. As he walked down Main Street, he greeted local store owners who were closing up for the day. He knew most of them on a first-name basis or just enough to stop and make small talk when he saw them. He really did enjoy small-town living.

He entered the Dead Crow and went straight to the bar. Will, a young hippy-looking kid, was serving. Joe ordered a PBR shot of whiskey with a burger and fries. Will told him to take a seat and that he would bring Joe his food when it was ready.

Joe always preferred the back booth, but he could see a bunch of people sitting in it, so he chose the next booth to them. He sat down, did his shot and took a swig of beer as a chaser. He put his beer down, sat, and waited for Will to bring over his food.

Not intentional, but he could hear the people talking at the next booth behind him. Normally, the music at the Dead Crow was ear-splittingly loud, but he guessed that with Nina away, Will had the music down to socially acceptable levels.

"Yeah, he's fucked," said one of the male voices.

'Totally fucked," said one of the female voices in agreement.

Joe wondered what this poor schmuck had done. Perhaps if he kept listening, he would learn more.

"They're really going to go through with it?" asked a second male voice.

'Oh yeah, totally dude," said the first male voice. 'They arrive at 6 pm tomorrow night."

"How do you know that?" asked the first female voice.

"Jessie works at the motel. She said they made bookings for 4 rooms via Expedia and then called to let her know they wouldn't get to town until 6 pm," said the first male voice.

'Oh shit! They are gonna fuck him up," laughed a third male voice.

"Oh for real," said the first male voice, "Guys like that don't travel all that way for shits and giggles."

'What did he do?" asked a second female voice.

"He killed one of their guys," said the first male.

"Oh damn," said the third male voice 'There is no way guys like that will turn up in force just to slap someone around."

"Hell no," said the second male voice 'People like that don't fuck around. We will probably get to witness a murder."

'Dude, it's not gonna be a murder, it's going to be a bloody massacre," joked the second female voice.

A murder? Thought Joe, *That poor sap. Whoever they were talking about. His goose was cooked.*

Joe took a sip of his beer and looked over to see Will, the hippy kid, walking over with his burger and fries. He smiled and took the plate from the young bartender. The Dead Crow Saloon was pretty much a shit hole, but their burgers and fries were amazing. He thanked Will and greedily took a bite out of his burger. As he was chewing on it, he strained to eavesdrop some more on the talk at the next table.

'Well, what did he do for them to come after him?" asked the first female.

'Well, check this," said the first male voice. "They were all down in Mexico, and they invited him to sit and have a beer with them."

"Okay," said the first female voice.

"Then he flips out over nothing, pulls a gun and shoots their club Vice President right in the middle of the diner," the first male voice explained.

'Whoa, what a scum bag. That's insane," said the second male voice. The other voices all agreed at once.

"No wonder they are coming for him," said the second female voice.

Joe felt sick. They were talking about his and Johnny's run-in with guys from the Dark Legion MC six months ago. He stopped eating. In fact, he realized he was physically shaking.

"It took them six months, but they finally tracked the killer down to Pine Hollow," said the first voice again.

Killer? thought Joe. *These kids have got it all wrong. It wasn't him who killed Kyle Ossi from the Dark Legion, but Johnny. This was all some big misunderstanding.*

"Well, sounds like tomorrow evening justice will be served," said the second male voice. "Pricks like that need to stay out of our town."

"Yes, so true," said the second female voice.

Joe had lost his appetite. His mind was going a million miles an hour. What to do? Pack up and leave town? Stay and stand his ground? Call the Steel Reapers for backup? Reach out to the Sheriff? He made up his mind there and then, he wasn't going to run, and he wasn't going to speak to the new Sheriff. Despite being out of the Reapers motorcycle club, he was old school and always felt that you never cooperate with law enforcement. But certainly staying and fighting meant certain death.

Somehow, he had to do something before tomorrow night. But what?

CHAPTER 2

Ryder was on his Harley, and he was heading down a road he had never ridden on before. The weather was warm but not too hot, with pine trees on either side of him. It didn't look like any road he had been on in the Inland Empire; maybe he was in Colorado? He couldn't be sure. He looked over to his right, and there she was. This older woman with the long, flowing hair. Who was she? It was weird; he usually dated girls in their early 20s, only a year or two younger than himself. Why would he be into someone almost the same age as his mom? He figured he would pull over, stop and talk to her. He blipped down through his gears before coming to a stop 100 feet up the road from her. He put his kickstand down and shut off his hog. The long-haired older woman started walking towards him. Who was she? He would soon find out. The first question was going to be her name, and the second question would be, "Are you stalking me?" He pulled off his helmet and walked towards her. As soon as he got closer enough, he said 'Hey, what's your name?"

Before she could answer, his alarm went off. Where was he? All of a sudden, he could hear his cellmate taking a piss. Ugh, reality came crashing back in. He had been dreaming. He was in his cell in California's notorious Sierra Crest Penitentiary. He had robbed a weed dispensary with his oldest friend in the world, Vince. They had gotten away. Vince had drugged him, left him unconscious in the rear parking lot of his local supermarket. He had woken up staring down the barrel of a patrolman's pistol. He was busted. They had caught him with some money from the dispensary. Vince had taken the majority of it and left him just enough to get a serious sentence. They put a lot of pressure on him to roll over on Vince. Despite his best friend throwing him to the wolves, he refused to snitch. That would be a sure death sentence behind the wire. The only thing prisoners hated more than child molesters were snitches.

Not working with the cops caused the judge to go hard on him. Despite having a string of small-time offenses under his belt, drug possession, assault, etc, they chose to make an example of him. 20 years. First place they sent him was the old school prison, Bayview State Prison, up in Northern California. Or as the locals called it, HELL VIEW. This was one of those places that the guards referred to as 'Gladiator school." Fights, usually organized and sanctioned by the guards, happened at least once a week. Deaths were a common occurrence, as were suicides or as the lifers used to call it, "Early Parole". Some people had a sick sense of humor.

Ryder didn't have a racist bone in his body, but Californian prison politics dictated that he had to stick with his own race. He resented that. When he first arrived at Hell View, the whites had worked with the Southern Mexicans but were at war with the Blacks and Northern Mexicans. Ryder thought it was ridiculous, but those were the rules. He had learnt quickly that the prison had its rules, but the prisoners' rules were more important to follow.

One upside to the crazy world of life behind bars was all the motorcycle clubs that he was at war with on the street. None of that bad blood carried over to the prison system, and he got to spend his days talking Harleys with many guys he would never be able to associate with in the so-called free world.

After serving 4 years in Hell view, he was jumped by a couple of new guys who had come in from a Federal Prison and were looking to shake him down. Instead of bending the knee to them, he fought, beating them both into a bloody pulp. Guards knew it was him, but the two dudes he had hospitalized wouldn't roll over. So Ryder scored no more prison time, but they transferred him back down south to Sierra Crest Penitentiary out in the high desert. It was a newer prison, with slightly better conditions, but more importantly, he was only an hour from where he grew up. Which meant his sister could come and visit him. This helped him deal with the time he was serving.

The first year of his incarceration, he turned his anger inward. Starting with smoking weed and drinking prison-made wine, Pruno. Made from fruit sugar and bread, it tasted awful, but you got a decent buzz out of it. He dabbled in snorting meth and smoking Heroin until one day he accepted the fact that these were just poisons, slowly sucking the life out of him. They didn't help; they hurt. After that, he cleaned up his act, ate right (well, the best he could behind the wall), and worked out. He lost count of the number of push-ups he had done in a day.

What fueled him now was simple. One word: vengeance. He was going to stay alive and do his time. Get out. Hunt down Vince and kill him. You fuck with me, then I fuck with you. No mercy, no clemency. What Vince did to Ryder was unforgivable. Before he died, he would get out of this living hellhole and find his former brother. Getting punished by a judge? That was one of the risks of committing a crime. Fighting with fellow prisoners? Sure! That could even be fun at times. Getting beaten up by prison guards? It sucked, but hey! It came with the territory. No pain from a beating could compare to the sorrow caused by Vince's betrayal. Vince would pay for this if this were the last thing that Ryder would ever do. Every morning and every night, he thought about hunting him down and destroying him. One day, he would get out, and one day Vince would die by Ryder's own hands. Of that he was sure.

CHAPTER 3

Modern Day Arizona.

B ack in Pine Hollow, Joe had to leave the bar. He walked back down Main Street in a daze. He felt like throwing up. Had there been any cars on the road, he would have probably been run over. It took him a minute to realize he was walking down the side of the street and not on the sidewalk. He corrected himself and got out of the road.

Why were the Lost Wolves after him? Did they know it wasn't him who killed their brother, but Johnny McIntire? Did they know Johnny was dead and that Joe was responsible? Is that why they were coming for him? Was this his penance for killing his best friend? He recalled reading once that every criminal who had been on the run for years and years, when they finally got caught, they were not mad, they were relieved. The years of running, hiding, and living with the fear that they were going to be caught by law enforcement at any moment weighed on them so heavily that it ate away at them. Getting arrested and facing the music was a weight off their shoulders. Was this what was happening to him? Was it God? Was it karma? He didn't know. He didn't even know what to do.

Somehow, he made it home. Joe wasn't a big pot smoker but did keep a small stash at home. It was legal, so why not? His nerves were so shot he figured a quick smoke of a joint might chill him out. Steady his nerves and clear his head. He had to come up with a plan of action.

He smoked a joint. One that Clay had given him was called a Jeter. (He assumed after baseball legend Derek Jeter?). His plan to relax and chill out had failed. The weed in this joint was 10 times stronger than what he was used to. Now his mind was going a thousand miles an hour as opposed to a hundred miles an hour. How had they known he was in Pine Hollow? He was no longer a member of the Steel Reapers. How had they tracked him down? Was there a snitch in town?

He would never go to law enforcement, and he didn't want to run. That said, he didn't want to die, shot down on Main Street either. What to do? What to do? The weed wasn't helping, just making him more and more paranoid. He needed to slow his brain down. Joe realized this was why he usually left weed alone. He got up off his couch and grabbed a beer from the fridge. Perhaps a couple of beers would slow his brain down.

He returned to his couch and pounded a few beers. Just over an hour had passed, and he was starting to feel calmer. He needed a battle plan. Perhaps he could face them and explain it wasn't him who killed their club brother? Maybe if he manned up, that would impress them enough to calm them down?

What if they didn't listen to reason? What if they had no code of honor? Most younger guys these days didn't have the same biker code of honor as the older guys; he couldn't risk his life on the possibility they would listen to reason.

Too many what-ifs? He had to reach out to someone.

Who was the kid who took over the Steel Reapers Phoenix chapter after Jon Jon retired? Spark? Striker? No, Spike! He had Spike's number somewhere; he could reach out to Spike and ask for backup. Yes, that could work. He grabbed his phone and started searching for Spike's number.

It took him a minute to find the Phoenix Chapter's president on his phone. Like a dumbass, he had saved Spike's number under "Phoenix Club Spike," and not "Spike." Didn't matter; he found the number and dialed it.

The phone rang. Finally, someone picked up.

"Yeah?" said the voice.

"Hey, is this Spike?" asked Joe.

"Yeah. Who's this?" Spike asked.

"It's Joe," he replied.

"Joe who?" asked Spike.

"Joe from the Steel Reapers, Spike! Ahh, what about "Moose," you would probably know me as Moose," Joe explained.

'Ah yeah, Johnny's friend! You were tight with Jon Jon before he retired, right?" asked Spike, warming up to Joe finally.

"Yeah, we came up with Jon Jon," said Joe

'Okay, I remember you now," said Spike, "How ya been?"

"Ahh, not so good," said Joe, "In fact, I need your help."

"Oh, okay. What do you need?" asked Spike.

"Ok, so the Lost Wolves are coming down from Utah or wherever to Pine Hollow to kill me," Joe explained.

"Pine Hollow? We have a motorcycle shop up there!" said Spike.

"Yeah, I work for Clay," said Joe

'Oh, that's cool," Spike replied.

'Well, it's not cool that they are bringing a death squad down to kill me, Spike," said Joe, eager to keep Spike on topic.

'The Lost Wolves? Pfft, I wouldn't worry, they're a bunch of fruit loops," Spike replied dismissively.

'Spike, I am worried. I'm not going to run. I am going to stand my ground, but I need help," said Joe, trying not to sound desperate.

"Okay, okay, calm down, bro," said Spike. "I will tell ya what. I'll talk to some of the boys and see if we can send you some help, okay?"

'Okay, thanks, man. Like I said, I'm not going to run, and I am not going to the cops. I just need some backup," said Joe.

"Don't sweat it, bro. I'll call some of the boys and get right back to you," Spike reassured.

'Okay, great, so when do you think I will hear back from you?" asked Joe

"Hmmm, I guess first thing in the morning? Cool?" said Spike.

"Okay, great, much appreciated, brother, thanks," Joe replied. They said their goodbyes, and Joe hung up with Spike. Well, that was something. At least with the Steel Reapers coming, he felt a bit better.

He finally calmed down enough to sleep. In fact, the combo of beer and weed made him super tired. Hearing that reinforcements were on their way had helped, too.

Joe prepared for bed, and before he knew it, he was passed out.

Joe woke the next day in a great mood. He put on his coffee pot and made some bacon and eggs. He had hope. That was all he needed. Just get some support from others, and he will figure out the rest when the Lost Wolves roll into town.

He had just finished his coffee and was getting ready to leave for work when his phone rang. He grabbed it and checked the number. It was Spike. Ahh, excellent, he thought, perfect timing. Sometimes the stars do align, and things go right for you. He flicked his phone to accept the call.

'Hey Spike, it's Joe," he greeted the Phoenix Club president 'How are things?"

'Yeah, things are pretty good here," said Spike. "How are you?"

'Doing much better since we last spoke," said Joe.

'Oh, that's good." Spike replied, "So listen, I rang around and spoke with some of the boys last night."

"Oh yeah?" said Joe, sounding hopeful.

'Yeah," Spike replied, "So, I had forgotten you were out bad with the club, man."

'What? No, I'm not out bad. That was Johnny!" said Joe.

"Yeah, but you left right after he did, didn't ya?" asked Spike.

'Yeah, I did. But I was told it was all good," said Joe, panic rising in his voice.

"Well, apparently not. Look, man, I heard you were a solid guy, but we can't just all leave our jobs and come to your rescue when you're out bad. Like you want us to do something for you, but what do you do for the club these days? Nothing man. I'm sorry, but that's our decision and we have to stick by it."

"Spike, no. I'm telling ya, man. I am not out bad," stammered Joe. He was starting to lose it.

"I'm sorry, man, our decision is final. I am sure you will be okay, bro. Don't sweat it," said Spike.

"Spike, no but..,"

'Hey man, sorry, I've got to get my ass to work. Hit me up if you're ever back in Phoenix, and we can grab a beer or something," Spike replied before hanging up on Joe.

Joe stood there for a moment, frozen in fear, staring at his phone. *So that's it? Discarded like a piece of trash after decades of loyal service to the club?* He felt sick again.

CHAPTER 4

Southern California.

The years rolled by. Ryder felt like he had lost his youth. Meeting a girl, getting married, getting a mortgage on a house, and having kids. All was lost to him. To make matters worse, one day in the showers, he was washing his hair, and strands came out of his hands; he was going bald. The stress of constantly having to be on high alert day in and day out had caused him to lose his hair prematurely. That very afternoon, he visited the prison barber shop and got his remaining hair shaved off. No more long hair for him. He grew a beard as well. Everyone said facial hair suited him. He had gone from long hair and a clean face to a shaved head and a big lumberjack beard. People who had known him a long time said he was virtually unrecognizable now. He was okay with that.

For the last 2 years, he had stayed clear of prison politics as much as he could. Obviously, he still had to fall in line with the guys on his cell block, but he kept his head down and tried to make the most of his time behind the wire. He managed to get on the kitchen staff at Sierra Crest, which afforded him the best food, and he took trainee electrician classes in the afternoon, too. He still focused as much time as possible on working out, keeping his body strong, which helped keep his mind strong. Along the way, he had seen so many better men than him fall to pieces under California prison conditions. Only the strong would survive.

As soon as he was up for parole, he applied. Both hearings, they let him speak for 30 minutes before the board told him 'Sorry, not this time". Ryder felt they had already made up their minds before he talked that they were going to refuse him, but they let him speak anyway. Giving him the false sense of hope that he may be set free. Fuck them then. He would do all his time if that's what was required of him.

It was very hard not to lose hope after so many years. Sierra Crest Penitentiary was full of stories of men who had been sentenced to relatively short terms and, by making poor decisions behind bars, got themselves life sentences or had o.d. on opioids. Ryder was determined not to go down the same path; the only thing keeping him sane and off the path of self-destruction was the thought of one day getting free. Tracking down Vince and extracting revenge on his former brother. Anger and hatred ate him alive, but inversely also kept him strong. He would get out of here, and he would find that traitorous prick.

One Tuesday morning, after kitchen duty, one of the guards came and got him. He was cuffed up and taken to a side building next to the administration building. To his surprise, he was informed by the warden that due to overcrowding in the California prison system, he was now going to be released. What had it been? 20 years. 5 more to go? He would still have to meet with a probation officer and not screw up for 12 months, but Ryder accepted. He was out the following afternoon.

He stood outside waiting for his sister to collect him. He was a different man now, older, wiser, but just as determined. He would do what it took to stay sweet with the probation officer and then track down Vince.

His sister and her husband had a small welcome home party for him. It was weird; he couldn't relax unless he sat in their small kitchen. Any other room in the house made him uncomfortable.

His first visit to the probation office was an eye-opener. His assigned officer, Mister Preston, was a middle-aged slob of a man. Totally disorganized. Papers and notes were strewn all over his cluttered office. Box files everywhere. The guy probably started off with the best of intentions, and years of government bureaucracy had worn the man down. Anyways, he seemed nice enough, although he told Ryder he had to seek gainful employment immediately or be sent back to prison.

Returning from his first visit to the probation office, he stopped off at the local healthy organic style supermarket and applied for a job on a whim. To his surprise, they called him the next day to give him a chance. Training was basic, but what he noticed was that they actually paid pretty decently and had a good benefits program. Things had changed since he was last out in the so-called free world. A supermarket job was one of the worst, low-paying jobs before Ryder had been locked up; now it was pretty competitive.

His sister had managed to save one of his motorcycles when he got locked up. It felt great to be back on two wheels after so many years away. Now he had a day job and a means of transportation. As soon as he could, he would set out to destroy his arch nemesis, Vince. Just keep his nose to the grindstone, build up some dollars, and he would be on his way. He had been through the worst life had to offer; this was the easy part in comparison to the last 20 years of living hell.

CHAPTER 5

Pine Hollow, Arizona.

Joe wasn't even sick now that Spike and the club had let him down. Half shock and half anger. He thought back to all the times he had come to the aid of a club member in need and never even questioned the circumstances. That was the code in those days. They called. You came. Then you asked what was needed of you. Such b.s. these days. He was never out bad. He had always done right by the club. This is how they treat him? After decades of loyal service? That was wrong.

He thought back to the early 2000s. Phoenix Club president Jon Jon had attended a "peacekeeping" meeting with one of the big clubs whose power base these days was in Florida. The meetings went very well, with a lot of progress made between the Steel Reapers and the then Illinois- now Florida-based MC.

On the plane ride back from Daytona Beach, Jon Jon noticed that there were 4 guys from the Daggered Souls MC Phoenix chapter on the plane. Economy class, of course. Jon Jon had used the in-flight phone (remember those?) to call the Phoenix boys to be armed up and waiting when his plane got into Phoenix's Sky Harbor airport that afternoon. Without even asking why, both he and Johnny had dropped everything and arrived on scene along with 6 other local Steel Reapers.

Somehow, the Daggered Souls boys had gotten word to their local people as well, and 2 hapless Daggered Souls members had walked right into Joe and Johnny on their arrival at the airport. They were beaten outside the airport in the dark recesses of the short-stay car park before even making it into the arrivals lounge. Once Joe and Johnny met up with the other Steel Reapers boys, they spaced themselves out discreetly all over the arrivals lounge based on which carousel the Daytona Beach passengers' luggage would be dispersed at.

The plane had apparently landed, and the Steel Reapers boys readied themselves for conflict. This was before the horrors of September 11th, 2001, when civilians could walk in off the street and have access to the arrivals lounge.

After a few minutes had passed, Joe figured the arriving passengers from upstairs had to be the people from Jon Jon's flight. The surfwear and 'Party at Daytona Beach" t-shirts were a dead giveaway.

As soon as Jon Jon spied Joe and Johnny waiting for him, he swung on the lead, Daggered Souls thug. Joe and Johnny charged the 3 other men. The remaining Steel Reapers leapt into action too as commuters screamed and scrambled out of the way of the ultra-violent melee. It was pure chaos. Even before 9-11, there was an unspoken feeling of safety and security at the airport. It was like having a brawl in a bank. It just wasn't the way polite society behaved. Punch out at a crusty biker bar? Sure, of course! Stabbing at an all-night gas station on the bad side of town? A slow night! A fight at an airport? Nationwide news.

The 4 Daggered Souls dudes were beaten viciously. Jon Jon, Joe, Johnny and 3 of the other Steel Reapers were arrested by airport security and taken downtown. They all stuck to the same story: the Daggered Souls had attacked them, and they were simply defending themselves. Much to Joe's surprise, the Daggered Souls club guys kept their mouths shut and refused to cooperate with the investigation. He respected that. A true old school criminal mindset. After a long trial and a bucket of money spent on lawyers, all 6 of the Steel Reapers were found innocent; they were free men.

Neither Joe nor Johnny had complained then – they did what was right for the club despite the financial and emotional ruin it had put on them both at the time. They didn't complain, they accepted it and got on with their lives. That was the life. Deal with it or patch out. Simple.

Now that he needed help, where were his "brothers"? Nowhere to be found. *Shitty way to treat an O.G. But hey, that's life,* thought Joe. It hardly seemed fair. He was left to face this crisis alone.

He ate some breakfast and tried to enjoy his morning coffee, one of the few pleasures in his simple life these days. After that was done, he actually wondered whether it was worth cleaning his dishes or not. Would he even have been coming back home tonight? If he were a betting man, he would probably bet against himself, but he decided to clean them regardless. Old habits die hard.

Joe debated riding his bike to town or walking. If he rode, they might target and destroy his beloved Harley in retaliation. But if he didn't ride, would that be showing weakness or defeat? He wasn't sure, so he figured fuck it. Ride it in. Maybe he could lock it up in the store's back room before they arrived?

He rode to work. The simple act of being on his bike helped clear his head. Maybe he should just take this as a sign and hit the road? He could be in Flagstaff within the hour, and Vegas, but late lunchtime. Sure, perhaps they would still find him, but at least it would give him time to think of a plan. Was that running? What if they were coming from Flagstaff and being caught on the open road, which made him an easier target? He decided he would stand his ground. *You run now, you will be running for the rest of your life,* he thought. Stay and face the music regardless of the outcome.

He arrived at Clay's bike shop on Main Street and opened up for today's work. He wheeled his bike through the shop to the back and placed it between two other Harleys that were due for servicing.

He was fiddling with the shop's sound system when he saw the Sheriff's car pull up. Oh, great. That's just what I need: law enforcement sniffing about. Joe had already made up his mind that he wouldn't talk to them.

Sheriff Williams entered his shop.

"How's it going, Joe?" the Sheriff asked.

"Oh, hey, Sheriff Williams, didn't see ya come in there," Joe replied.

"Clay is away, right?" asked the Sheriff.

"Yes, Sir, down in Mexico with his girl Nina," Joe replied.

'That's good. Nina's a good soul," said Sheriff Williams. "They make a good couple."

'Yes, they do," Joe replied.

Sheriff Williams nodded and continued to browse through the motorcycle shop.

"You looking for anything in particular, Sheriff?" asked Joe.

"Yeah, I was considering buying a Harley again," Sheriff Williams explained 'I used to ride back in the day," he explained.

Everyone used to ride back in the day, thought Joe, *who cares? Didn't matter if you used to ride; it only mattered that you still ride now.*

"Oh yeah? That's cool," said Joe. "Looking for anything in particular?"

'Yeah, actually," said Sheriff Williams, "A good quality Dyna Wide Glide with low mileage."

'Hmm, I might have a source for one of those Sheriff," said Joe, "Mileage under 50000 would probably set ya back $7000 or so, if that works."

"Yeah, that could work," said the Sheriff. 'Let me know, okay?"

'Will do, Sheriff," Joe replied. Anything else?"

"Ah yeah," said the Sheriff, clearing his throat 'It's come to my attention some rival club is coming to town tonight to teach you a lesson."

"Club? What? This is news to me," said Joe in mock disbelief.

Sheriff Williams gave him a look that said YEAH, RIGHT.

"Well, regardless of whether you already knew or not, I won't tolerate any club violence in my town," said Sheriff Williams sternly.

"Well, this is news to me," said Joe, not very convincingly 'What do you suggest I do?"

'Well, look. When Clay and his boys turned up in town, I wasn't the Sheriff. We knew you guys were all one percenters, and we ignored it. So far, Clay and his guys have not given us any trouble.

I don't appreciate that 6 months after you arrive, we are getting dragged into a potential biker war," said Sheriff Williams.

'Okay," said Joe. 'So what do you want me to do?"

"I want you to take it out of town," said Sheriff Williams. "There is a big field 2 miles out of town. Meet your pals there and sort out whatever beef you have with them away from Pine Hollow."

"Ahh, but..," Joe started.

"Look, trust me, I know these club wars are common. Whatever you guys want to do to each other, well, that's your business. But I cannot sit back and allow some poor high school girl or whoever to be shot by one of your guys," said the Sheriff 'So I am asking you, take it out of town, okay?"

Joe was shocked. He was secretly hoping for police protection or at least back up. 'So, you're not going to help me? ' he asked, barely concealing his panic now.

'Help you? I have already told you – no one in town wants anything to do with your club politics. You guys choose to live that way? Hey! That's fine. This is America. I say live and let live. But do not bring your wars to my town. Do you understand?" snapped the Sheriff.

"Not really, no," said Joe at a loss for words.

'Just take your beefs and your wars and settle that shit out of town. OKAY?" said the Sheriff, making a hasty exit to the front door of the bike shop.

The Sheriff left Joe feeling more scared and confused than ever before. He had no plan. He needed a plan before the guys turned up.

CHAPTER 6

Southern California.

Ryder came home from another day working at the supermarket. He was beat, exhausted. He made sure never to show any emotion at work. An irate customer was complaining that the cookie aisle had been moved to another part of the store, screaming at him. No problem. Some grandpa telling him that the price of a bag of potato chips was 50 cents when he was a kid, and why was everything so expensive these days? No problem. Just nod and agree with them and get through another day. What was the point of screaming at them? What would be achieved by beating the stupid old man senseless? That would just get him back inside with even more annoying people. The worst of the worst. You think the outside world is bad? Every single annoying personality trait was magnified on the inside. He had seen people stabbed for feeling up the food in the chow line to get the best apple or banana.

That said, you could only bury your emotions deep down inside for so long before they came bubbling back up. In his previous experience, it all came out in epic proportions. He had to get out on the road and start tracking down Vince before he blew it and assaulted an annoying customer. He took stock of everything in his life.

He was 45 years old. No wife, no kids, staying on an inflatable bed in a small room in the back of his sister's and her husband's suburban home. That sucked. But then again, many guys who get out have no support system; heck, some even commit a crime just to get thrown back inside. At least then they know where they stand in life. Locked in a cell 23 hrs a day, getting told what time to get up, when to eat, when to work, when to go to sleep. He got it, but swore he would never become one of those guys.

What did he have going for him? He wasn't hooked on drugs; he didn't even drink anymore. He hadn't let himself turn to a big slab of lard, which was easy to do with such terrible food behind the wire. He had a job, and he knew from firsthand accounts that most guys had trouble getting a job once they were outside and fell back into their old ways of wheeling and dealing. Not him. He still had one Harley left. As long as he had his scooter, did he need much more?

He was 3 months into his probation. He was still having to do random piss tests, but that was easy since he wasn't doing dope. He had managed to save some money from his job. He paid his sister a small amount, more of a token gesture for rent and saved the rest. He ate simply, and with the discount he got from work, his grocery bill was nothing compared to that of the average person. He didn't own a car, he didn't have a gym membership, and he wasn't paying alimony to an ex-wife who hated his guts and poisoned his kids against him. Judging from the stories he heard on the inside, this was more common with most men his age than not. So he had that going for him.

So, according to Ryder's calculations, he was doing better than some and worse than others, right smack in the middle. So what was the plan? Save some more money, get probation behind him and then head to Arizona and hunt down Vince. It wasn't even the money that Vince had stolen from Ryder or the amount of prison time Ryder got that really ate him up. It was the principle. If he had gotten 6 months in prison from Vince's treachery, or if the amount had been $500, it would still hurt just as badly. That said, seeking revenge had fueled his entire twenty-year bid. If he didn't have that on his mind, he would probably still be locked up inside or worse, dead from an overdose.

He was getting ready to use his sister's kitchen to make something to eat when his phone rang. He checked the number; it was his probation officer. Weird. He wasn't due back for 3 more days yet. Had he messed up? Ryder didn't think so. He took the call.

"Hello?" he said

"Ryder, this is Mister Preston. How are you doing?" the voice said.

"Hi, Mister Preston, yes, doing good. In fact, I just got home from work. Everything okay?" Ryder asked.

'Yes, yes. Hey, real quick, can you make it into my office tomorrow?" asked his probation officer.

Ryder checked his work schedule on his phone. He wasn't needed in until 12 pm tomorrow.

"I can do any time before 11 30 am Ryder replied. "Something wrong?"

"Ok, good, can you swing by at 10 am? Won't take long," Mister Preston replied. Ryder noticed he hadn't answered his question about something being wrong.

"Ok, see you then," said Ryder.

"Great, bye," said Mister Preston, hanging up on Ryder before he could ask any further questions.

Ryder sat there for a moment, his plans to start dinner thwarted. Why was he calling? What now? Was he being sent back to prison? He tried to think if he had messed up in any way and came up with nothing.

The next morning, Ryder took his Harley and cruised over to the probation office with the plan of going straight to work after seeing Mister Preston.

As usual, there was a complete rogues' gallery of criminals sitting in the waiting room. Ryder cast his eyes over the room to see if he recognized anyone from the penitentiary. He didn't.

It was 10.30 am before he was called in. Typical government-run office. Nothing was ever on time. It was a good thing his place of work was only a 5-minute ride away from here.

He knocked, waited until he was called in and walked into Mister Preston's office. As usual, the place was an explosion of files and paperwork over every corner of his office. Without looking up, Mister Preston greeted him.

"Hello Ryder, how's work going? The probation officer asked.

"All good, thanks for asking," Ryder replied. "Is there some kind of problem?"

"Problem? No, no problem, quite the opposite," Mister Preston explained.

"Uhh," said Ryder, fairly confused.

"Look, my case load just doubled, and I was already overworked and underpaid," Mister Preston said.

"Yes, you look very busy," said Ryder, surveying the man's office.

"You have come in repeatedly with a clean piss test. You are holding down steady gainful employment," said Mister Preston.

41

"Well, I'm trying my best to turn my life around," Ryder started to explain.

"Yes, I can see that. And I greatly appreciate your efforts. Which is why I called you in today," said Mister Preston. "So if it's okay with you, I would like the rest of your probation term for you just to call in once a week. You don't even need to speak to me if I am busy. You can speak to my receptionist, Tracy."

Uh, okay, um, cool," Ryder replied.

"Just answer her questions and make sure you call in every Tuesday morning, say 10 am. Okay?"

'Wow, great, thanks, Mister Preston," said Ryder.

'Look, you've done great work so far. Don't screw up, okay?

'Don't worry, I won't," Ryder replied.

"Okay, great. Any questions?" asked Mister Preston.

"No, no. No questions. Thanks for putting your trust in me," said Ryder.

"Okay, very well. All the best and good luck," said Mr. Preston. "Now, if you don't mind, I have some work to get on with."

"Thanks, Mister Preston," said Ryder, getting up and shaking his probation officer's hand before exiting the office.

Ryder's head was spinning. He was kind of free. What now? There was only one clear answer. Time to hunt down that traitor, Vince.

CHAPTER 7

Pine Hollow, Arizona.

Joe was shook. He decided to lock up shop and go up the street and get some more coffee. He walked up Main Street and waved at the old couple who owned the Thrift store two doors up from Clay's bike shop. Normally, they would wave back or even come out and shoot the shit with him for a couple of minutes, but today, they just looked at him like he was a ghost, then turned away. Joe shrugged it off; they clearly had other things on their minds.

He passed the town hardware store next and saw Old Man Flanagan sweeping the floor. He waved at the old geezer, too, and he just looked down and didn't respond. *Weird* thought, Joe. *Everyone's in a bad mood today,* he figured.

He made it up to the Pine Hollow Breakfast Club, his "go-to" diner. The Tanner family owned the place and were always happy to see Joe when he came in for breakfast or lunch.

He approached the counter and asked for a cup of coffee to go. Their daughter, Sharlene, looked at him, didn't say a word and walked away from the counter. *Again, weird.* Moments later, her father appeared at the counter. She had obviously gone and fetched him.

"Howdy Joe," greeted Mister Tanner.

"Hey Frank, coffee, please," asked Joe.

'Yeah, about that, no offense, but can you go elsewhere today, please?" asked Mister Tanner.

"Are you all out?" asked Joe, somewhat surprised since most of the other patrons seemed to have fresh coffee on their tables.

"Look, Sheriff Williams came and saw us this morning. He advised us to stay clear of you, at least for today," Mister Tanner explained.

'What on earth?" asked Joe, totally taken aback. There must be some form of mistake.

"Joe, listen to me," said Mister Tanner 'It's nothing personal, in fact, I like you a lot. You know that"

"Okay..," Joe started to reply.

"I have a business to run and a family to support," explained Mister Tanner. "I know you seem like a good guy, but we can't be involved with shootouts with rival biker gangs."

"But..," Joe started to reply yet again.

'Maybe you could try up the street at that sandwich place," Mister Tanner suggested.

"But," said Joe.

"I'm sorry, man, like the Sheriff warned us. We can't afford to get involved, Joe," said Mister Tanner, looking down at the floor and not directly at Joe.

'I just want a cup of coffee," was all Joe could manage to blurt out.

"You can try up the street, Joe. Sorry, the Sheriff told us not to serve you. No offense," said Mister Tanner.

Joe turned to leave. Why is it that people would say the most offensive or obnoxious thing to you and then add 'No offense" if that was meant to make it alright? How many other people had the Sheriff warned off serving Joe? No wonder the Thrift store couple and old Man Flanagan had blanked him. Sheriff Williams definitely spoke to them.

He had walked the two extra blocks to the sandwich place. The coffee here wasn't great, and it was a distance from the bike shop, but what choice did he have?

He went into the sandwich shop to see the shiftless teenager who often worked the counter staring at his phone.

"Coffee, please, milk, no sugar," asked Joe.

'Soy or Almond?" asked the kid.

"Huh?" asked Joe. Soy or Almond what? He wasn't getting a candy bar.

"Soy or Almond milk," said the kid, not taking his eyes off his cell phone.

"Regular milk is just fine," Joe replied.

"2% or fat-free?" asked the kid.

'Normal, full-fat milk if ya got it," Joe snapped back.

"Oh, okay," said the kid who went off to fetch Joe's order.

"$2 please," the kid said, still not looking at Joe.

Joe paid the youth and took his coffee. The kid finally looked at him.

"Ohhhhh, it's you!" he exclaimed.

"Yes, it's me," said Joe. *What was this kid talking about?*

"Can I get a selfie with you?" asked the teen.

"What? Why?" asked Joe.

"Uh, just cuz," the kid replied somewhat nervously.

'Sorry, kid, I don't have time. I gotta go," Joe replied. "See ya soon."

"Yeah, I doubt it," the kid said under his breath as Joe walked out of the establishment.

CHAPTER 8

Southern California.

Ryder thought back to the first time he met Vince in elementary school. They had to have both been 10 years old at the time. Vince was the new kid, and he and Ryder had bonded over their love of the Batman animated TV series.

Both of them had come from dysfunctional families. Ryder's dad had cut out on the family when he was 3, and Vince's mom was on about her third husband. Vince's older brother was much older (10 years, Ryder thought) and had problems with drugs and booze. It seemed as far back as Ryder could remember that Vince's older brother was in and out of jail. Vince and Ryder had become surrogate brothers – they were there for each other when no one else was.

Once they got to know each other, they found out they both had more than Batman in common. Each of them had extensive GI Joe action figure collections, which were rare for their generation of kids. It was more Batman and the Power Rangers in the early '90s. Ryder had inherited his from his cousin, and Vince from his older brother. Both of them became obsessed with the military and swore that when they got old enough, they would join the Marines. They would always be playing soldiers in abandoned buildings and vacant lots. Abandoned buildings were war-torn

France, and Vacant lots were exotic jungles deep in the heart of Vietnam.

At age 12, they scored a couple of used nonfunctional gas masks from the local Army and Navy surplus store and would spend their weekends wearing the masks and crawling around on their hands and knees in the local overgrown vacant lot. Hours of fun.

In High School, they were more concerned with parties and meeting girls than studying. Who needed to study anyway? The plan was to join the armed forces as soon as they turned 17. Weekdays were spent daydreaming about the weekends, and by Thursday afternoon, they knew whose parents were out of town and where the best parties would be. At that point, most of the kids in their class were still listening to the Grunge bands of the day, Nirvana, Sound Garden and Pearl Jam. Some pop punk and skate punk stuff got played at parties, too. Ryder and Vince both grew their hair long and rode Honda Rebel motorcycles. As soon as they joined the military, they would buy Harleys. That was the plan.

Vince turned 17 first. 6 weeks later, Ryder did. They went down to the army recruitment office and told the recruiter they were ready to sign up. First up was the written tests. Ryder felt they both passed with top scores. In the afternoon, they were given physicals again, and Ryder felt they both passed with ease. They did more tests on them, such as push-ups, pull-ups, etc. Since both of them had been training for years for this very day, they were again top scoring. Finally, after 7 hours of being run through the ringer, the Army Sargent took them into his office.

"Okay, boys, I've got good news and bad news," the huge military man explained to them. "You both passed your aptitude tests and your physicals with flying colors."

Ryder and Vince looked at each other excitedly. This was it, this was the moment.

"However," the recruiter continued.

There was always a "However," wasn't there? Thought Ryder bitterly. *Both of them had criminal records for minor offenses, petty theft, underage drinking, etc., but nothing that would show on their adult records.*

"Due to your non-conformist haircuts, we are going to have to pass on accepting you both. We wish you all the best in the future. Good day"

The military man got up and opened the door to his office to show them out.

Non-conforming haircuts? Thought Ryder. *What is he talking about? They had long hair. Wasn't that day one of basic training? They shave your head and make you a skinhead?*

Ryder thought back on that day. How ironic. He was now shaving his head anyway.

To add insult to injury. A few years later, the USA would invade Iraq, and military recruiters were taking anyone with a pulse. If they had applied, then they would have been accepted for sure.

CHAPTER 9

Pine Hollow, Arizona.

Joe went back to the bike shop. How did that kid hear about the Dark Legion guys coming to town? Did everyone know? Was that Sheriff spreading the news? Maybe he really should cut and run? If he did cut and run, how long before word spread and they found him again? Back in the old days, he was confident he had enough connections to get him a brand new fake Social Security number, driver's license and passport. These days, he was out of touch with those types of people. Sooner or later, no matter where he ran, they would surely find him.

He was right to stay. But what for? To get shot dead by these creeps? He didn't even kill the guy in Mexico; Johnny did. Maybe they would listen to reason? Talk it out with them? It was risky, and besides, who's to say they wouldn't start shooting first and ask questions later?

That's what happened in the old days of the wild west. He couldn't take the chance. He was so spooked he had trouble thinking clearly. There had to be a course of action where he didn't run but didn't end up bleeding out with a broken body full of bullets. What to do, what to do.

He sat on the office couch and finished his coffee. Still, no clear course of action came to mind. He recalled a success coach once saying that sometimes you don't have a clear idea of the outcome, but as long as you take some form of action, it is better than just sitting there and procrastinating.

He had to get a gun. He had sold his last collection a few years ago, back in Phoenix, when he got stung with a large tax bill. He had earned pretty much the same amount each year back then, and that year he got stung with a massive $3500 tax bill. How on earth did that work? Joe guessed that he had to raise everyone's tax rate to pay for all of those living on Welfare. Not wanting to get on the wrong side of Uncle Sam, he had to sell off his gun collection to get the bill paid promptly to avoid all the penalties.

Joe checked his wallet. $280. He could probably get a used Taurus 9mm for under $200 with some ammo at the Pawn shop. What was the old saying? Better to have a gun and not need it than need one and not have it. Yes, that's what he would do. Shut up shop again, walk the 6 blocks up Main Street to the pawn shop, and see what they had on offer.

He posted a "back in 5 minutes" sign on the door of the motorcycle shop and locked up. He turned and headed back up Main Street towards the Pawn Store. Hopefully, luck would be on his side, and he could score a nice little used 9mm for a decent price. He felt pretty good about his decision. At least it was something, and it might help him stay alive,

He passed a few locals on the way up to the pawn store. He made a point of saying "Good Morning" to each and every person he passed, old or young, male or female. Not one person replied to him. In the past, every single one of them would have greeted him, heck, even stopped and chatted with him. Had the entire town turned on him now? If so, weak sauce. If he were to survive this day, he would remember this.

He saw Old Man Hale sweeping the sidewalk in front of his pawn shop as he approached the block it was on. Hale stopped sweeping and looked up at him. Joe responded by waving. Mister Hale stopped sweeping and slipped back inside his pawn shop.

Must have had to take a call, thought Joe. When he made it to the store, he saw a sign in the window, "Closed."

"Oh come on now, are you kidding me?" Joe cursed. He tried the door. Nope, locked.

He knocked, lightly at first. He could see movement in the back of the shop.

"Come on, Mister Hale, I know you're in there," he shouted 'I saw you go in."

He started knocking louder now. "Cmon, man, open up."

Still nothing.

He started thumping on the glass now. He was concerned that if he wasn't careful, his fist would go right through the glass.

Finally, he saw Mr. Hale appear in the back of his shop. He looked red-faced and somewhat embarrassed. He unlocked the door.

Before Joe could walk in, Mister Hale came outside and quickly shut the door to his shop behind him.

"Hello Joe," he said somberly.

"Hi, Mr. Hale. How are you today?" Joe asked the old timer.

"Ah, very busy," Mister Hale replied gruffly.

"Busy is good, right?" asked Joe.

"Yes, I guess. Can I help you with anything? asked Hale.

'I would like to make a purchase from your fine establishment, sir," Joe declared.

"Sorry, Joe, not today," Hale replied.

"I won't be long, I promise," said Joe.

"Sorry, uh, it's inventory day. Have to do a stock check," said Mister Hale rather meekly. He wasn't fooling anyone.

'Oh, cmon, man. It's quick money for you. I won't be long. I swear," Joe pleaded.

Mr. Hale looked up and down Main Street. At that moment, there was zero foot traffic in Pine Hollow's main thoroughfare.

"Sorry, Joe. I can't," Hale replied.

"Oh, let me guess, Sheriff Williams had a word with you?" asked Joe.

'Well, he did warn us there was trouble coming, Joe," said Mister Hale.

"Dammit, Mister Hale, you know I have nothing to do with this. You have to believe me," Joe snapped.

"No need to use curse words, mister," said Mister Hale, turning around to head back inside.

"Look, I'm sorry, Mister Hale. I am telling you, I am an innocent man here, and I have the right to protect myself," said Joe.

"Maybe so, Joe, but look, people who live in this town. We are here for a reason. We stay out of those big crime-ridden cities like Flagstaff and Kingman. There's a reason we live here and raise our families here. It's safe and it's quiet. We want no part in gang warfare and violence," Hale explained.

Big crime-ridden cities? Flagstaff and Kingman? Boy, this guy had no clue, thought Joe.

"I just need to make a quick purchase from you, Mister Hale; no one needs to know it came from your shop," begged Joe.

"I'm sorry, son. I gave Sheriff Williams my word. I have to stay out of this."

Mister Hale turned his back on Joe.

"Cmon, Mister Hale, you are basically handing me a death sentence. PLEASE," said Joe, giving it one last try.

"Why not get out of town? Or try a Pawn shop in Flagstaff, Joe?" asked Mister Hale right before he closed the door on Joe's face.

It was useless. The man was scared, and he wasn't going to budge. Maybe Joe could get to Flagstaff and back in time?

CHAPTER 10

Southern California.

Killing time at his supermarket job, Ryder thought back to the days after getting rejected by the army. Both he and Vince had thought of nothing for years but joining up and becoming soldiers, and now with that dream crushed, they were just running wild. Work during the week has him at an Auto parts store, and Vince works as a trainee screen printer at one of those custom t-shirt places that little league teams would go to for merchandise. Their weekends were spent cruising around town and partying. Beer and weed were their go-to drugs. Well, maybe the occasional tab of acid too, but no hard stuff.

Saturday afternoon, they would go downtown and hang out in front of the local record store. Vince and Ryder were both hard rock guys, but it seemed that everyone in their town back then was all about pop punk stuff like Rancid, Face to Face and the Offspring. Ryder didn't love those bands, but they didn't irritate him either. The bonus was that every cute little punk rock chick really loved those bands, and that's where they would meet girls and find out where the parties were happening that night.

The weekend parties were usually a lot of fun for the duo. Some rich chick on the right side of town, whose parents would be away for the weekend, and a party would happen. Invariable, the 30 or

40 people who were invited would spread the word, and next thing you know, 300 to 400 kids would turn up. The liquor cabinet would get raided. The house would get trashed. Hearts would get broken. Fights would start, and ultimately, the cops would be called. Ryder lost track of the number of times he and Vince would have to flee in the night through suburban neighborhoods to avoid going to jail. Often, they would park their bikes a block or two away for that very reason. Always have an escape plan!

One Saturday afternoon, they were sitting on their Hondas when an older dude pulled up on a 1957 Pan Head Chopper.

"Nice bikes, fellas," said the older biker. In hindsight, now the guy was probably only 25 years old.

"Thanks," said Ryder.

'You do all the customization yourselves?" the older biker asked, admiring their handiwork.

"Yeah, pretty much," Vince replied, "We are learning as we go."

'Yeah, that's the good thing about those used Honda Shadows; they are relatively cheap. Great bikes to learn on."

"As soon as we can, we are buying Harleys," Vince added.

'Very cool," said the older biker. 'What's your name?"

Vince and Ryder introduced themselves. "I'm Chomps," said the older biker.

'Chops? As in Chopper?" asked Vince.

"No, choMps," explained Chomps, emphasizing the M.

"Oh," said Vince, looking confused.

"Apparently, I am a really loud eater; that's how I got the name," said Chomps. "Although personally, I don't hear it."

'Ah, ok," laughed Vince.

"My club is going for a ride next Saturday if you want to come. To the Ocean and back," said Chomps.

"Oh, cool. What club?" asked Ryder.

'I ride for the Iron Ravens," Chomps explained. "It's a good group of guys, and you are both more than welcome to ride with us," explained Chomps.

"Sure, sounds good," said Vince. "Where and when do we meet up?"

"There's a dive bar on Second Street called The Raven's Perch, do you know it?" Chomps replied.

Ryder thought about Second Street. There was a storefront church on the corner of Marshall Blvd and Second Street.

"Is it near the church?" asked Ryder.

Chomps thought for a minute, "Yeah, across the road and down two stores, from memory."

"Yeah! I think I know the bar you mean," said Ryder.

"Okay, be there no later than 10 am next Saturday," said Chomps.

"We will be there," said Vince, shaking Chomp's hand.

The run went great. It was both Vince and Ryder's first time on a group ride, and despite having to ride near the very back of the pack, they were both instantly hooked. The feeling of forty riders moving as one down State Route 91 was like nothing either of them had ever felt before—the Noise, the rush, the power. The fully patched members of the club both took a shine to the two young riders, and soon they were invited to parties at the Iron Ravens San Carmelo clubhouse. If Ryder and Vince had fun at high school parties, then this was on a whole other level.

Before Vince and Ryder knew it, they were both hangouts. Basically, a hang around was someone who was not a patched member or even a prospect yet. The point of being a hang around was for the club to get to know you and for you to understand what the club was about. It was the first step in joining an Outlaw Motorcycle club.

Think of it as, say, an "Observation," period. Are you the right fit for the club? Conversely, was the club the right fit for you? It was all about proving loyalty to the club. Both Ryder and Vince were expected to show commitment before they could ever be trusted with club business.

It was finally decided that both were "prospect worthy," material for the Iron Ravens. Then the real work began. They were pretty much on call 24-7, running errands and building relationships with the rest of the San Carmelo Iron Ravens.

Ryder saw it as a "Rite of Passage" to become an Iron Raven. One of the biggest takeaways that they both learned from Chomps was that a biker's strength lay in loyalty and brotherhood. Ryder found that this was something that had been missing in his life and was just as important to him as motorcycles were.

During their prospecting period, Ryder and Vince learnt the importance of supporting the families of brothers who were behind bars. Most men had wives and kids, and trying to run and maintain a household while their husbands were doing time behind the wire could be incredibly stressful for some of these ladies. Ryder and Vince were often instructed to go over to a brother's house and do things you wouldn't even think of as part of the Outlaw Biker world.

Mow the lawns, clear the gutters, paint a garden shed, and do small things that could really help a person out. The last thing a brother needed on the inside was a wife who spent all of her visiting time freaking out as their house was falling apart.

Another thing they were taught as prospects for the Iron Wolves was helping out in the funeral process for fallen brothers. A biker's funeral was a HUGE event for the Iron Wolves. Ensuring that their deceased brother was remembered in death as he was in life. Sometimes the party for a brother who had moved on to the other side could last for days and be talked about for years.

The key takeaway for all this in Ryder's mind was that it meant standing by your brother when it mattered, not just when there were beers to be drunk and parties to be had. Brotherhood was all.

In his mind, if he had committed the crime and gotten caught, and Vince hadn't come to visit him, that would be wrong. But the fact that his own brother, even long before they had joined the club, had thrown him to the wolves, was unforgivable. You do not come back from something like that. Vengeance would be Ryder's.

CHAPTER 11

Pine Hollow, Arizona.

Joe checked the office computer for Pawn Shops in Flagstaff. From what he could tell, it seemed like they had 4 or 5 of them across town. He wouldn't have time to browse them all, so he checked their ratings and chose the one nearest to the freeway with 5 stars. Lucky U Pawn. That would have to do. He had just enough time to ride there, grab a pistol, return and figure out a battle strategy.

He grabbed a pen and paper and wrote a note, "Back at 2 pm,". He retrieved his scoot and wheeled it out front. Joe quickly locked up the shop and fired up his bike. Soon, he was on the highway heading North towards Holbrook. No sooner had he hit the open road than he started to feel better. He guessed this was what meditation was like. All the stress and worry of the last 24 hours lifted. He felt good, no great. How was that possible? Maybe the Sheriff was right? Maybe he should just cut and run? He could drift from town to town for the rest of his life. Was that the solution? No. Joe was always taught as a kid 'You don't run from your problems. You stand and face them. Running away only ever made things worse. He would go to Flag, pick up a pistol and return. Of that, he was certain.

Joe thought back to the first time he visited Flagstaff. It was his first run with the Steel Reapers as a fully patched-in member of the club. Their annual Tucson to Flagstaff run. If you drove it in a car, you could make it in 4 hours or so. With a bunch of dudes on scoots? Eh, try 6 hours. Peanut gas tanks on bikes looked cool, but you were pretty much forced to stop every 100 miles to gas up again. Add a bunch of men who needed to hit the restroom, buy snacks, take a smoke break, and each gas station stop added another 15 – 20 minutes to the journey. But as they say, isn't that half the fun of a club run? Not the destination but the ride there? That had to be true. Half the time, more stories were shared years later about chaos at the truck stops and roadside diners than about whatever event they were attending.

Flagstaff was different, though. It was primarily a big college town at the time, and it was the first time Joe had sex with two different girls in one night. Many men say it's the club patch that attracted ladies like white on rice. Others argued that the patch gave the man the confidence that impressed the women. Some say it was the pheromones from having sex with the first chick that attracted the second one. Whatever it was, it worked for Joe that crazy night. He knew he didn't have male model good looks, and he was never one of these guys who were naturally charming and witty to women. So it had to be one of the theories that made that night so memorable.

Other than banging two chicks in one night, it was the very first time Joe and Johnny got to meet and hang with guys from the Steel Reapers Nevada and Utah chapters. All super cool guys. Joe recalled meeting one of the Nevada guys 10 years later, and the guy remembered Joe from the party. Joe had asked him, "How was the party?" to which the guy replied, "It was great, I woke up face-first in a storefront doorway two blocks away the next morning, freezing my ass off!" That was pretty much the yardstick for a good party in those wild and crazy days.

He was now nearing Flagstaff, so he swung into the right lane, ready for his exit. Unlike most riders these days, Joe preferred to read the road map before he left and figure it out from there, versus everyone else who solely relied on their GPS to guide them around, even if it was just to the local bar and back. *What was up with that?* he thought. *People are too lazy these days.* He and Johnny had travelled the entire country by bike. In the old days, relying only on fold-away maps to find their way, maybe they got lost once or twice, but wasn't that half the adventure? Of course, they always got to where they were going, eventually.

After a couple of twists and turns on surface roads through Flag, he found the pawn store. He parked up and went inside. He quickly located the gun counter and started looking at what they had on sale. He saw a couple of decent-quality Glocks and a Sig Sauer. He asked the staff member to pull those out of the cabinet for him. He checked the grip and weight on each, even dry-firing the Glock 19 and the 43.

The 19 felt right, so he asked the price. The guy wanted $500 for it. Way more than he could afford right now. He didn't have time to hit up every pawn store in Flagstaff. Joe also knew he couldn't leave empty-handed. What to do? What to do?

"Hey buddy, what can I get for $200?" asked Joe, half expecting a wise ass answer like "You can get the fudge out of my store, buddy," from the clerk.

The clerk looked deep in thought for a moment.

"Hmm, might have a few more in the back. However, I feel that when it comes to a pistol for home defense, you don't want to skimp on quality when it comes to your and your loved ones' lives. You know?"

'Yeah, yeah. I take your point, but it's also better to have any gun than no gun in some situations, wouldn't you agree?" Joe snapped back.

"Yes, true. Give me a minute, I'll be right back," The clerk disappeared into the back room.

Joe waited. He checked his watch. He was running out of time. How long did it take to hit the gun cabinet back there and sort through what else they had?

Finally, the man returned. It had probably only been 3 minutes, but it felt like a lifetime.

"Here you go, sir," the clerk said, laying out 3 more pistols on the countertop.

Two were straight garbage, but the third was an old and battered Taurus that promised possibilities.

He picked it up and tested the weight. He checked the iron sights and the action on it. Finally, he dry-fired the pistol.

"Okay, I like this. How much for the Taurus?"

$150 for that one, sir," the man responded.

"Ok, I'll take it," said Joe

"Do you need ammo, sir?" asked the clerk. "I can do you 50 rounds of full metal jacket 124 grain for $17 if that fits your budget?"

"Ok great, I'll take the lot," said Joe, fishing out his driver's license and handing it to the staff member.

It took the clerk a further 15 minutes to write up the paperwork and get Joe out the door. He shoved the pistol and ammo into his riding vest and fired up his Harley. He had to get back to Pine Hollow and formulate a plan. Joe made short work of the surface streets and was once again on the highway heading east back towards home. As he enjoyed the ride back to Pine Hollow, he morbidly wondered if this would be the last time he would ever ride his bike.

CHAPTER 12

Southern California.

Today was the day. Ryder had called his probation officer and spoken to the man's receptionist. She sounded bored as he confirmed, "Yes," he was still working. 'No," he wasn't taking drugs. "Yes," he was still being a good little robot and "No," he wasn't breaking the law all over in a matter of 90 seconds. If it was going to be this easy moving forward, then that was fine by him.

He had told the supermarket that he had to leave for a week for a family emergency. They were pissed off, but it was one of the few excuses that most employees still respected and didn't question. Fine by him. If he wasn't back in a week, he would either tell them the trouble was ongoing or risk getting fired. The only overriding thought in his mind was finding Vince and extracting revenge on his former best friend.

His plan was to travel to Phoenix, which was approximately 5 hours East of him. There, he would hit the most popular biker bars for a week or two and ask around about Vince. Despite being millions strong, the biker world was very tight and close-knit. If Vince were still in Arizona, someone in Phoenix would know. He would find the rat.

Ryder lashed a go bag to the sissy bar of his Harley. Inside, he had a small "on the road" tool kit with some ratcheting wrenches, a tire repair kit, electrical tape, a handful of fuses, some commonly used sockets, a 6-in-1 screwdriver and a stack of clean clothes. Time to hit the road.

It didn't take long before Ryder was in top gear, barreling down the I-10 heading East to Phoenix. He had done this run once before he had been incarcerated. It had been a mandatory club run for the Iron Ravens, and Ryder's first time out of the state. If you have never been in a pack of 30 riders all riding 100 miles per hour with only inches between each bike in tight coordination, you have no idea what an intense rush you feel. It was like being at an air show where the jet fighter pilots fly by at top speed. Ryder had not felt anything like that before. Riding solo towards Arizona again, well, it wasn't the same fleeing, but it sure felt good. He had missed 20 years of that due to the traitorous behavior of that rat Vince.

An hour into his ride, and he was in the High Desert. Ryder thought about the early pioneers coming out here in covered wagons. They had no clue what was ahead of them and how long it would take to reach the coast, yet they persevered. Balls of steel in his mind. People were cut from a different cloth back then. No room for moaning and complaining. Shut up and get on with it, or perish. Perhaps that's what was wrong with today's world, people just had it too damn easy.

He found a gas station in Joshua Tree and topped up his tank, stretched his legs and grabbed a soda to hydrate. His lower back throbbed slightly, and his shoulders felt sore. He was clearly out of practice with long rides, and yet again, he blamed Vince for this.

He killed his soda and tossed the can in the trash. Ryder hated people who littered. No respect for their surroundings or other people. Sheer weak-willed laziness, in his opinion. He fired up his

Harley and rolled back out onto the I-10 freeway and resumed his journey to Phoenix.

It felt great to be on the open road, sun beating down on his arms as he rode. He felt sorry for those stuck in trucks and cars as he wove in and out of traffic. Those people were missing out, and they had no clue how much more real it felt to ride without a cage. You truly experienced all the elements riding your bike versus sitting in a car.

Ryder pulled over in the town of Blythe, about two hours east of Joshua Tree and about 2 hours west of Phoenix. He figured he would be a good spot to gas up, stretch his legs, sit down and eat a good meal. He found a diner and headed inside. Most of the customers looked up when he walked in and went straight back to eating their food. Good. *Leave me alone, and I will leave you alone* thought Ryder.

He felt better after a good meal and some iced tea. Ryder figured he probably had 2 hours to go until hitting Phoenix. From memory of his last visit there, he figured he could ride the I-10 all the way into downtown and then head north on the I-17 to Sunnyslope, then up Cave Creek Road to the Filthy Hogg. The Iron Ravens had booked and taken over an entire low-budget motel back then. He wondered whether he would be able to find the same motel or not. Probably torn down by now, he thought.

He paid for his lunch, took a piss and went back out to his scooter. He checked to make sure nothing had shaken loose in the last two hours, and after giving his bike the once-over, he pulled on his helmet and fired up his scoot for the next leg of his journey.

Close to 90 minutes into the final leg of his ride, traffic started to thicken up. It had probably been close to 25 years since he was last in Phoenix, but he was amazed at how much the city had grown. What had once been farm land was now sprawling suburbs. Where did all these people come from? The North East? California? Other countries? He didn't know, but he was both impressed and concerned that maybe the Filthy Hogg was no longer where he remembered it to be, just north of Sunnyslope on Cave Creek Road. There were more biker bars in the town of Cave Creek; perhaps he could check there if the Filthy Hogg was gone.

As he got closer and closer to downtown, traffic was really building up. Ryder guessed it had to be close to 4 pm and not even rush out yet. Felt like Phoenix was getting more and more like Los Angeles than his last visit all those years ago. He managed to find the exit for the I-17 North and was relieved to be off the 10 before some idiot, more concerned about texting on his phone, ran him off the road. Before he got locked up, they used to say drunk drivers were the biggest danger to motorcyclists; now it seemed it was cell phones. He assumed that 99.999% of all the calls and texts that people were doing were not crucial, life-saving calls, but just silly nonsense. You're gonna kill a biker by being distracted looking at the latest shopping trends on Insta Book or whatever the latest app that everyone used was called.

Ryder saw the exit for Northern Ave. It was a road that ran West to East, dissecting Phoenix. He recalled they had used Northern Ave last time to get to the Filthy Hogg. Unlike Los Angeles or Boston, where Freeways were like someone dropped a plate of spaghetti on the floor, Phoenix was more similar to New York City, where everything was laid out in a simple grid fashion. So much easier to find your way around when the town planners had thought ahead.

Ryder racked his brains trying to remember if it was North 7th Ave or North 7th Street that got him to Cave Creek Rd. What was it the Iron Ravens club president had told him all those years ago? West of town, it was Avenues North to South, and after Central Ave, East of that, it was Streets. It had to be 7th Street and not 7th Avenue that would take him North to the Filthy Hogg Saloon.

Ryder passed Central Ave and swung into the left lane in preparation for turning left. The next set of lights turned out to be North 7th Street, and he took the turn, riding up the wide suburban shopping road. It was funny that even though he had only been here once before, how much of the street he did actually remember.

He rode a couple of blocks at the speed limit, keen not to miss the turn off for Cave Creek Rd. This must be Sunnyslope now, he thought. Some of the run-down apartment buildings looked familiar to him, or was it just a trick of the mind?

He passed a McDonald's on his right, but there was still no sign of the turn off for Cave Creek Rd. He came to the next set of lights, and there it was. Cave Creek Rd forked to the right from North 7th, and he swung over and raced up the wide street. Yep, kind of like he remembered it. Motorcycle shops, thrift stores, auto yards and biker bars. The Filthy Hogg was somewhere along here on the right, but where?

Ryder nearly crashed his bike when he saw it. It was funny how your memory worked. He could remember some things in such detail, but when he got there, it was actually a few blocks further north than he had pictured it in his mind. To be fair, he had been following his club brothers from California and was probably at that time more concerned with not crashing into the rider in front of him than taking mental notes on each landmark from California to Phoenix.

Regardless, he had found the place. He was about to find a decent spot to do a U-turn when he saw a run-down motel half a block ahead. This wasn't where they stayed during their last visit, but if he had to hole up in town for a few days to track down Vince, then this might work for him. He blipped down in gears and turned into the motel courtyard. He parked out front of the head office and went inside. The room rate was reasonable, and he managed to get a room on the ground floor so that he could roll his bike inside. He recalled even back in the day, some of these cheap Phoenix motels had sketchy people hanging around, and the last thing he needed was for some crack head to steal his bike.

He pushed his bike into his room and dumped his bag on the bed. He walked back to the front office, where he had spotted a few vending machines, and grabbed some bottles of water and some munchies for later. He returned to his room, dumped them on his bed and decided to take a quick shower and change out of his dirty clothes. Feeling refreshed, Ryder decided a quick power nap would help. When he woke up, it was dark outside. He decided to leave his bike and take a walk down the street to the Filthy Hogg Saloon and have a drink or two. He vaguely recalled that they did serve some basic bar food and was hoping that was still the case 25 years later.

When he hit the infamous bar, he noticed there were only seven bikes parked out front. One panhead and there were a couple of bobbers, or like the hipsters called them these days, "Bar hoppers". Was that an oxymoron or what? He couldn't think of anything worse than going from bar to bar getting progressively more wasted while trying to ride your bike. Oh well, each to their own, he shrugged.

He bought a beer and a whiskey shot from the well-developed barmaid and then looked around. A couple of old barflies are sitting in the booths, and there are no real obvious 'biker' types. What the heck? Then he remembered there was a patio out back. He found the back door that led outside and took his beer and his shot with him. There, he found a bunch of young bikers sitting at various tables. A couple looked up when he walked out, but paid him no mind.

He found a table and sat down with his back to the wall so he could see immediately anyone who walked out from the bar. *Where were all the old timers?* From what he could tell, most of these riders were in their early 20s; he needed older guys who would know of the Iron Ravens. Still, Ryder figured it wasn't all a waste of time. If he just showed up out of the blue and started asking questions, people might figure him for a cop or even worse, an informant. It wouldn't do his credibility any harm if he were seen around the bar for a couple of days before he found the right people to help him with his search. So he sat and enjoyed his beer, listening to the rock music blasting through the bar's speaker system. Some songs he recognized, but a lot he didn't. He had been out of the loop so long that there was a whole generation or two of bands he had missed out on by being locked up.

At the end of the night, he had put away at least 4 beers and 2 shots. Nothing like his drinking ability before he got put away, but 25 years of no access to booze will turn you into a lightweight. That was okay; he wasn't trying to impress anyone; he just gathered intel on that rat Vince.

CHAPTER 13

Pine Hollow, Arizona.

Joe got back to Pine Hollow and reopened the store. It was now after 4 pm. Supposedly, these pricks were getting to town right on 6 pm. He didn't know how this was established, but he had to work on the idea that they may turn up late or early. After all this rushing around back and forth to Flagstaff, he still hadn't come up with a plan.

Taking on board the warnings from Sheriff Williams and not wanting to destroy poor Clay's bike show, he had accepted the fact that he couldn't stand his ground here. Imagine Clay's face if he returned from vacation to find his shop burned to the ground and ransacked. Not good. Clay had given him a break, and he didn't want to let him down.

Joe figured he would leave a message on the door, telling the Dark Legion goons that he was a mile down the road at the clearing outside of town. At least that way, no townspeople would get dragged into their beef. He would close up in 5 minutes and get on site and figure out a more fleshed out plan then.

All of a sudden, he had the urge to call his ex-wife Veronica. Just in case he didn't make it back from this, he should call her and make amends. Just clear the air and tell her how he felt.

Better to go out on a good note, not a bad one, he figured.

He grabbed his cell phone and found her number. He hit call. The phone rang. And rang. Finally.

"Hello?" a voice said.

"Hey, it's me," Joe said.

"I'm sorry. New phone, who's this?" she asked.

"Joe!" Joe replied.

'Which Joe? I know a lot of Joes," she asked. Was she doing this on purpose? He used to be the number 1 Joe in her life. She should know his voice after all these years.

"Your ex-husband," he snapped.

"There's no need to shout. What do you want, Joe?" Veronica replied.

'I just wanted to check in and see how you are doing," said Joe.

"I'm fine. Why are you really calling?" she asked.

"Like I said, it's been a while, and I figured I would reach out to you," said Joe.

'Bullshit. You only call when you want something from me," Veronica grizzled.

"No, no, I don't want anything from you. Look, here's the deal. I am facing a situation I might not come back from, and just wanted to reach out to you," said Joe

Veronica sighed. "You and that stupid gang. Don't you remember why we divorced?"

Joe could feel the tension rising in his body. Veronica always had a way of pushing his buttons.

"It's not a gang, it's a club. Besides, you know damn well I left the club," Joe replied somewhat unconvincingly.

'Yeah, right. If it's not a gang, why are you in trouble then?" Veronica questioned.

"Look, it's all a big misunderstanding," Joe replied," I just wanted to tell you, we had some good times."

"Good times? You've got to be kidding me. I wish I had never met you," Veronica snapped.

"Oh come on now, you don't mean that," said Joe.

"I do mean it. You and your stupid bikes wrecked my life. I could have done so much better than you."

Joe sighed. She used to love his bikes. When they had first started dating, she almost begged him to always bring his bike and not his truck. What was the old saying? "The woman you divorce is not the woman you married." That was definitely him and Veronica.

'Don't say that," he said to her softly. Too late, she was going into full rant mode.

"I told you 100 times. That stupid patch on your back will be the death of you," she ranted.

Oh boy, here we go, thought Joe.

'Men fighting and killing each other over a $5.00 patch on their backs? Pathetic,"

"Look, I told you it's not the cost of making a patch, it's way, way more than that," said Joe.

"Yeah, right. So that's why guys are coming to get you? You just never learn, do you?" Veronica continued.

"I am out of the club. It's not about the club. It's a big misunderstanding," Joe replied.

"Bullshit. People talk out misunderstandings, they don't arrive in a big posse to kill you, do they?" Veronica spat back.

Joe remembered why they divorced now. She was such a ball breaker. She always wanted emotional (and of course, financial) support from him, but when he needed anything from her, all he got back was anger and accusations. Life was too short to live like that.

"Well, that's my plan. To try to make them see that they are wrong," said Joe.

"But if you fail at that, like you do with everything in your life, they will kill you? Yeah, it sounds like a misunderstanding to me," Veronica said, snipping at him.

Dammit. This was just like her. Always had to twist everything up and make it worse. He was starting to wish he had never called her now. He was now more stressed out than the thought of facing the Dark Legion thugs.

"Look, I gotta get going," said Joe. "I just wanted to call and wish you a nice life."

'Well, I wish you hadn't. Look, just don't call me again," Veronica grumbled before hanging up.

Wow, thanks for the support. Bitch. Joe shook his head. He now felt worse than before the call.

Veronica was good at that. Getting inside his head and throwing off his focus and concentration. With support like that, who needed her? He could see now why he preferred the brotherhood of the club versus being married to her. No club brother of his would ever dream of putting him down like that. Fuck it.

75

CHAPTER 14

Sunnyslope, Arizona.

This was the third night in a row Ryder had been hitting the Filthy Hogg. He had ridden out to some of the bigger biker bars in the town of Cave Creek early evening yesterday, and they were both fairly dead, too. He figured most dudes saved the big boozing sessions for the weekends, when they could sleep it off the next morning and not have to worry about messing up their jobs.

Tonight was Thursday night, so maybe he would have better luck than last night. He left the motel with low expectations as he didn't want to set himself up for disappointment. To his surprise, arriving at the dive bar, he saw about 30-40 scoots parked out front. *Okay, so maybe tonight WILL be different.*

Ryder entered the bar and was immediately surprised by the difference from Wednesday night to Thursday night. The juke box was cranked up, and pretty much every booth inside was taken. He had to shout over the counter for the barmaid to hear his order. As soon as he got his beer and his whiskey shot, he went outside. He couldn't hear himself think with all that noise, and he had zero chance of chatting to someone over that racket. Perhaps 20 years ago, he would have enjoyed it, but it was too much for him now.

He hit the patio and found a spare table. No sooner had he done his whiskey shot and taken a sip of beer than an older guy called out.

"Hey, Red, don't I know you?"

Ryder assumed he must be talking to him.

"Me?" he asked, pointing a finger at himself.

'Yeah, you," said the geezer, picking up his beer and inviting himself to Ryder's table.

Ryder looked the guy up and down. He didn't look familiar. 'I don't think so"

'Sure you do," smiled the biker, "Let me think."

The man paused like he was doing a math problem in his head.

"I know I have seen you before. One second," he paused 'Oh, I got it. Sierra Crest? You were in C block, I think."

'D block," Ryder corrected him.

"Ahh, I knew it. I am terrible with names, but I never forget a face," the man said. "Oh, let me introduce myself. I'm Dave," the biker extended his hand.

Ryder took it and shook the man's hand. "Nice to meet ya. You can call me Red."

Cuz of the red beard? Yeah, figured as much. I think you were getting transferred in as I was getting out," Dave explained.

'Very cool, how long have you been living in Arizona?" asked Ryder.

"As soon as I was done with probation in California, I got the hell out. Start again, somewhere new. Besides, California ain't what it used to be," Dave added.

77

"Yeah, I hear that," said Ryder. Dave finished his beer, and Ryder went back inside and picked up two more beers and two shots. Dave could prove to be useful. A couple of beers and then he might loosen up a bit. Ryder returned and placed a beer and a shot in front of Dave.

"Oh shit, thanks man, that's very kind of you. I'll get the next round," Dave offered.

"So what about you?" he asked Ryder.

"Eh, I'm just passing through. Hitting the road after I finished my probation," Ryder explained.

"Yeah, I feel that, man. First thing I did when I got out was buy a new bike," said Dave.

They shot the shit for a while longer, talking about the pros and cons of Arizona versus California. Dave even went and got them a round of drinks too,

Eventually, Ryder put it to him.

"Hey, man, I was wondering if you could help me?" he asked.

'Sure, bro, what do you need?" Dave asked.

"I'm trying to track down an old buddy whom I haven't seen in over 20 years. Last I heard, he had moved to Arizona."

'Sure, man, what was his name?" asked Dave.

"Vince and I used to ride for the Iron Ravens back then," said Ryder.

"The Iron Ravens?" whistled Dave 'Damn, that's a legit club." Ryder could see that Dave was impressed.

'Yeah, not as big as the Steel Reapers in AZ, but we held our own in California," Ryder said.

'That is true," said Dave. "So Vince was an Iron Raven, yeah?" asked Dave 'When did he move to Arizona?"

"Yeah, last I saw of him, he was a Raven, but I doubt he is anymore. None of the California boys has heard from him in over 20 years," said Ryder.

'Oh, out bad is he?" asked Dave.

"Well, not really, he just packed up and left. No one knows what happened to him," said Ryder.

"He snitch on somebody or something?" asked Dave.

"No, nothing like that," lied Ryder, "I grew up with him, just looking to re-connect."

"That's very cool. Let me go ask Sparky, he's out front. If anyone at the Hogg would know it would be him," said Dave. I'll bring you a beer when I get back,"

Dave got up and went back through the bar.

Ryder sat there thinking. Well, this sounds promising. Maybe this Sparky guy knows where to find him. He took another sip of beer. As soon as he put his glass back down on the table, a guy at the next table sat down.

"Hey, man, JC. Nice to meet ya," said the wiry young biker, extending his hand. "You're an Iron Raven? Man, you guys are legends."

"Thanks," said Ryder, shaking the dudes hand, but thinking *I don't recall inviting you to sit down.*

"Can I get you a beer or anything?" asked JC.

Ryder looked at his glass. He had about two gulps to go. What the hell. Why not?

'Sure, thanks, man," said Ryder.

JC got up and went to the bar. JC returned with two beers and two shots. At this stage, Ryder was glad that he had left his bike back in his motel room and had not ridden to the bar. The last thing he needed was a DUI from the Phoenix cops when he was meant to be lying low in California.

The duo did their shots and sipped on their beers. Ryder couldn't help noticing that JC looked a little like a much younger version of himself. Was it the eyes and nose? Either way is uncanny.

"Hey, so I heard you are new in town. If you need a gun or anything, let me know, I can hook it up," offered JC.

"Nah, I'm good," said Ryder, "Although I do love Arizona's common sense gun laws. I'm not looking for a pistol right now."

"I can get you a really good price on a brand new Glock, brother," JC once again offered.

"Thanks, but no thanks," Ryder replied.

'What about Coke? You need some cocaine?" asked JC

Ryder thought for a moment. He was starting to get pretty buzzed. He hadn't drunk this much in over 20 years. In the old days, he could drink all night without issue. He was definitely out of practice. Maybe some Coke would help straighten his head out.

"Eh, no thanks, JC. At my age, my heart would probably explode if I did coke," Ryder explained.

"Nah nah. It's super clean stuff. Fresh over the border, you'll love it," JC replied.

'Hey. Thanks for the offer, but I am good for now," said Ryder.

The pair spoke some more with JC, asking a bunch of questions about the Iron Ravens.

Ryder took a moment and cleared his head. What was up with this guy? Rule number one in the club and prison: someone asking too many questions, someone offering you all sorts of contraband? One hundred percent a fed boi or an informant. How had he missed this? He was getting sloppy. He would have smashed this kid on sight back in the old days. He decided to test him out.

'So, Glocks, eh?" asked Ryder.

'Yeah, yeah, brand new man," said JC eagerly.

"If they're brand new, how come they're so cheap?" asked Ryder.

"Ahh, let's just say they fell off the back of a truck," smiled JC.

"Ah, got ya," Ryder replied. 'What are we talking about here? My funds are pretty limited."

Hmm, for you, a Glock 17 Gen 5? I could do $100!" JC replied.

Ryder thought for a moment. A Glock 17 easily goes for $500 or so. What was the old saying? Does it sound too good to be true? It usually isn't true."

"Hmm, that's a pretty sweet deal. Maybe later on," Ryder replied.

"You got it, buddy," smiled JC, "Hey, you need another beer?"

Ryder looked at his nearly empty glass. "Sure, why not?"

JC went up to grab more beers for them both.

Ryder looked around for Dave. No sign of the guy. Was he full of shit? Did he leave? Ryder was disappointed that Dave had been his best lead so far and was hoping he would have some solid intel. Maybe he had gotten his hopes up over nothing.

JC returned with two beers, passing one over to Ryder.

"Here ya go, brother," said JC

"Thanks, man, next round is on me," Ryder replied.

Ryder was getting bloated with all this beer. Halfway through this pint, he went to fart. All of a sudden, he realized that if he tried to fart, he was going to shit himself. What the hell? He always took a morning dump; he couldn't remember the last time he had to go in the evening. He got up quickly to find the restroom.

"Hey, I'll be right back," he said to JC before scurrying off back inside the saloon.

Ryder quickly found the restrooms. There were 4 stalls and about 8 urinals. He took the stall at the far end of the restroom, the one farthest from the door.

He just about finished his business when he heard someone come in. Taking a dump in prison was usually when you got attacked, as it was pretty much your most vulnerable time. He tensed and listened.

Whoever it was went straight for the pisser. He let him self relax slightly. He could hear the man washing his hands, then drying them. Ryder had just finished his business and was pulling his jeans back up when he heard the guy leave. Seconds later, someone else entered the restroom.

'Hello? Hello?" said the voice. "Anyone in here?"

Instead of answering, instinctively, Ryder, ever so quietly, raised his legs so he could squat on the toilet seat. He could hear the guy coming down the row of stalls, and he imagined the dude was peering into each. Coke user, possibly? That said, with the clientele at the Filthy Hogg, you could probably rack some lines out on your table and snort to your heart's content, and no one would say anything. Ryder was curious to see where this was going.

Clearly satisfied no one was in the restroom, the nameless person made a phone call. Ryder listened in. he could only hear this side of the conversation.

"Yeah, it's me," the voice said.

'Yeah, I think I got one," the voice continued, "Gimme 30 minutes and make sure you have some people stationed near my truck, be ready."

The voice sounded like that wiry dude JC's voice. It was JC's voice. The guy was a rat. But who was he talking about?

'Yeah, definitely a felon, Iron Ravens MC, I'm telling ya," JC continued.

That fucker was trying to set me up! Fumed Ryder. He had heard stories about professional rats. Paid for by law enforcement to entrap people and send them to prison. Pure scum. Lower than low.

Very carefully, Ryder lowered his boots to the floor. He undid the latch on the stall door and listened.

'Yeah, I gotta go, just be ready, okay?" said JC before hanging up his phone.

Ryder could hear the rat washing his hands. Time to strike. Ryder moved fast and silently. At the last second, JC looked up from the sink at the washroom mirror. The look of complete fear on his face lasted a split second before Ryder rammed the rat's head into the wall with full force. He heard the sickening crunch of cartilage and bone as the man's nose crashed into the wall.

"No!" was all he managed to say before Ryder cracked the informant's head repeatedly into the wall. JC collapsed to the ground, his face a bloody and broken mess.

83

Ryder kicked the man in the ribs a couple of times for good measure. He had to leave before the cops wondered where their rat got to. He bent down and rummaged through JC's pockets. He found his wallet and rifled through it. Jean Claude Thomson. $500 in his wallet. No doubt, play money given to him by whatever agency paid him. "Asshole tax," Ryder figured, pocketing the bills. He grabbed his license too, just in case and swiftly exited the restroom before anyone else came in.

It was time to get out of town before Phoenix police caught up with him. He pushed through the crowd in the bar to get to the front door. He was almost there when he heard someone shout.

"Hey, Red!" Ryder looked back, and it was Dave pushing his way through the crowd to catch up to him. *Was he an informant to? Maybe he was JC's handler, working as a team to set up poor unsuspecting bikers.*

"What?" Ryder snapped at the older biker.

"Hey, good news. I got a lead for you," said Dave.

"What? You do?" Ryder wasn't expecting that.

"Yeah, head North, all the best, brother," said Dave, shaking Ryder's hand and slipping him a piece of paper.

'Thanks, man, you're the best," said Ryder, pushing through the front door.

Ryder slipped through the customers, trying to make their way into the bar. He had to control himself now so it looked like he was leaving casually and not in a hurry. He let his eyes scan across the street, looking for undercover cops. There was a florist van parked across Cave Creek Road, and a couple of cars too that could possibly have cops in them. He pretended he wasn't staring at them and walked at a relaxed pace back towards his motel. Had he told JC where he was staying? He didn't think so. Should he pack and leave now? He wasn't sure. He couldn't afford to go to jail right now; he had to find Vince.

Safely back in his room, he examined the piece of paper Dave had slipped him. It said the following: *"He's out past Show Low in one of the towns on the road to Snowflake".* Despite the buzz he had from all the beers, Ryder grabbed his paper map and unfolded it over his motel bed. There were 4 towns between Show Low and Snowflake. How good was this intel? Had he moved on? Was he living as a recluse in a shack like the Unabomber? Was this a needle-in-a-haystack situation? He didn't know, but he did know he probably wouldn't be welcome in Phoenix anytime in the foreseeable future.

Ryder decided he was too drunk to leave tonight. If the cops were out looking for him now, it would be a bad time to leave. He would sleep it off and leave at first light the next morning. He figured he could spend a week in each of the 4 towns, hit every bar in the area, get to know the locals, and sooner or later someone would know what had happened to Vince. The beauty of small towns is that pretty much everyone knew everyone else's business, and someone somewhere would have an idea or a memory of Vince and some idea of where he was. This was the best lead he had had in 25 years, and he wasn't going to blow it. He cleared all the junk off his bed, and within minutes, he had passed out.

CHAPTER 15

Las Vegas, Nevada.

KC rolled out of bed. He was in a cheap motel off the Las Vegas strip. His body ached; he was still sore from yesterday's ride. It had taken him and the boys 9 hours to ride down from Richmond, California, to Las Vegas. As the newly elected national president of the Dark Legion Motorcycle Club, this mission was important to him. One of his men had been killed on a road trip in Mexico by a scumbag from the Steel Reapers, and now it was his time to shine. He couldn't be seen to let it slide. What message would that send to other one percent motorcycle clubs? *You can do anything to our guys without having to worry about retribution?* No sir. Not on his watch. Justice would be served by his own hands.

The club had been searching for about six months to hunt down the scum who shot poor Kyle in cold blood right in the middle of a diner, off the beaten track deep in Cartel country, by a Steel Reaper of all people. Those guys were old and stale. They might have been one of the premier clubs in the 80s and 90s, but they were pretty much considered the 'Over the hill" club now. A club like the Dark Legion just letting one of their guys get killed in cold blood by some old fart? Unacceptable.

They had their support club guys scour all of Arizona, hitting every dive and biker bar in the state looking for intel. For months, nothing. It seemed like an impossible task. His boys had given a pretty good description of the shooter, and to KC's shock, last week, they had a confirmed sighting of the killer working in a small motorcycle shop in a town in Northern Arizona called Pine Hollow. He had never heard of it, but it looked like a good 6 hours out from Vegas.

KC had grown up in a small town just outside of Humboldt County in Northern California. He had been riding bikes since his 6th birthday, when his dad gave him a Honda Grom. At 18, he had become a hang around for the Dark Legion MC and started prospecting for them at age 20. At 21, he became a full patched member of the club and quickly rose through the ranks. He had moved south to the club's headquarters in Richmond, California, to be closer to his newfound family.

Richmond was a funny place. If you rode over the Bay Bridge from San Francisco (one of the most expensive cities in the entire USA), you could turn right to go to Berkeley, a hive of wealthy liberal people or turn left to go to Richmond, which was impoverished and extremely dangerous. There used to be a saying that people who couldn't afford to live in San Francisco felt sorry for themselves for living in Oakland, but were thankful they didn't have to live in Richmond. That's how bad Richmond was. However, the Dark Legion was so well established there, with such a reputation for violence, that locals gave them a wide berth. Their compound by the bay was left alone, and so were all their visitors. The locals knew if you messed with one of them, you took on the whole club.

They were due to meet with Mike, Johnny and Frank, 3 club brothers who were in attendance when Kyle got murdered at that diner in Mexico. KC had given word to some of the younger people in the town of Pine Hollow that the Dark Legion was coming to seek vengeance. The way Kyle saw it, half the secret to winning the war was to break the enemy's spirit long before you started the fight. By announcing your arrival, sure, there was a risk that your foe would run, but even if they did, it would eat them up for the rest of their miserable life. No matter where they went, how far they traveled, they would be looking over their shoulder, expecting you to jump out from behind a wall or a tree. They could lie awake in bed at night just seeing your face, knowing you would not stop till you caught them. You would mentally break them before they were physically broken. KC had studied tactics of war all his life, and the Steel Reapers would pay for that, as they did to his family.

CHAPTER 16

Pine Hollow, Arizona.

Joe grabbed a piece of clean paper and a Sharpie marker pen. He wrote as best as he could on the paper, "Dark Legion, I am waiting for you 2 miles south of here. Take Main Street out of town until it becomes Harper's Road. There is a big car park on the left-hand side. No guns or Knives. Joe"

He taped the sign to the inside of the shop window and did a quick check of the shop before locking up. At least if he died this evening, Clay's shop should remain intact. That was the best he could do. He made sure he had his pistol in his riding vest and fired up his motorcycle. Was this his last ride? He tried not to think of the worst-case scenario, but in the pit of his stomach, he felt that this really could be the end. He took his sweet time coasting out of town, on his Harley, trying to savor every last moment.

It wasn't very long before he arrived at his destination. He wasn't sure if this was intended to be a rest stop for tourists or perhaps a soccer ground for the kids in town; heck, it might have been both. A planned rest stop turned soccer field. Regardless, it had a decent-sized car park and a wide open field surrounded by tall pines on two sides and a farmer's property to the south. Joe parked his bike to the side of the car park, but as close as he could get to the pines as possible. The Dark Legion would obviously still see his scoot but might be less likely to fuck with it being out of the way.

Joe walked into the middle of the empty field and stared back at the car park. They would clearly come from that direction. There was no chance that any of them could sneak through the tree line and sneak attack him.

He wondered what to do with the pistol. If he wanted to get into an open shoot-out with the Dark Legion, without a doubt, they would win. Joe had no idea how many were turning up, but he imagined at least 3 guys. They could all be bringing AKs for all he knew. His best bet was to plead to their sense of honor and fight it out man-on-man with fists. Showing his pistol right away would just escalate things. He could stash it somewhere and use it as a last resort.

He searched for a suitable hiding spot and decided his best bet was the path that led to the farmer's field. There was an old wooden post there; he could hide his pistol there and grab it as a last resort.

It wasn't much of a plan, but that's all he had.

CHAPTER 17

Pine Hollow, Arizona.

Sheriff Williams was pissed off. Damn one percenters. He had no problems with guys who rode motorcycles; in fact, he rode 'em as well in his wild and crazy youth. Guys who joined "Outlaw" clubs were basically putting a target on their backs. Attracting unwanted attention from both law enforcement AND other knuckleheads in other one percenter clubs. He didn't need that sort of aggravation in his life. He was voted in as sheriff of Pine Hollow after the previous Sheriff, a man named Calvin and his douchebag brother Dan were found to be running a vast Northern Arizona crime ring. Good riddance to those two as well. The last he heard, they were both doing state time in Florence penitentiary, some hellhole between Phoenix and Tucson. Right where they belong, as far as he was concerned.

He was a businessman first and foremost, and he had visions of building a legal empire all across the Highway 77 corridor. He had bought the Dead Crow saloon years ago and turned it into a profitable business, making enough money to open a family diner in the next town over. His sister in law, Leanne, ran the Copper Canyon Cafe and was already making great money for him and the family.

The way he saw it, with so many people moving to Phoenix from all over the country, some of those souls would find the summers way too hot and start to look for getaway homes in Northern Arizona. He planned to capitalize on that. Arizona was a great state with a lot of opportunities. Northern Arizona was the future, as far as he was concerned. In fact, he was banking on it.

Having violent shootouts with lawless hordes of bikers WAS NOT the future he saw for the town of Pine Hollow. That damn fool Clay, opening the bike shop, had caused a lot of these problems. Well, to be fair, he was okay with a motorcycle shop; he had visions of Pine Hollow becoming a destination for two-wheeled travelers from all over the nation, flocking to Pine Hollow as a summer riding spot. That part would do great for the economy and his plans for growth. Hiring that old geezer Joe with his connections to one-percenter gangs was the real problem.

Sheriff Williams figured he would swing by Clay's motorcycle shop around 530pm and see if the old fool had taken the hint and gotten out of town. If he wasn't going to run, then at least have his brawl with his rivals on old man Duggan's land. Technically, that was out of city limits, and if the shit really did hit the fan and this made the Arizona news, it wouldn't be tied to the town of Pine Hollow. He was thinking ahead. He was thinking big.

If Joe was still in town, Sheriff Williams figured he could always arrest him, then take him 10 miles out of town and dump him out there. By the time the fool walked back to Pine Hollow, things would have hopefully calmed down. Maybe he could even tell these out-of-town bikers where he had dumped old Joe, and they could do what they had to do far, far away from Pine Hollow.

Sheriff Williams looked at the clock on the wall and the stack of paperwork on his desk. He had about 30 minutes to get through filing all these expense reports before he had to shut down the station and go check on Joe. He cursed the old biker. He had far better things to do with his time than step in between a biker gang war.

CHAPTER 18

Sunnyslope, Arizona.

Ryder woke up. At first, he thought he was still in his cell at Sierra Crest Penitentiary before realizing he was in his motel room. Sometimes he felt he had post-traumatic stress disorder from all the violence and insanity he witnessed during his time behind the wire. Even the violence he inflicted on others to survive weighed heavily on him. No man should see such things.

Ryder remembered the first week he spent in Bayview State Prison. A child molester was put in a solitary cell. He was kept locked up 23 hrs a day on his own behind bars (For his own protection); however, instead of being fearful and keeping a low profile. This sack of shit went out of his way to torment and goad the other prisoners when they walked past his cell. Ryder figured this guy felt safe as he was behind bars, and the rest of the people in the cell block had no access to him. One morning, as they were all heading to the chow hall, the molester was doing it again, jeering and goading the main line prisoners. A con about 10 people ahead of Ryder sprayed a liquid from a small bottle between the bars all over the pedophile and the creep's cell. Then a prisoner right in front of Ryder flicked a lit match into the cell. The sex offender was burned alive in his cell. Sometimes, late at night, lying in bed, Ryder could still hear the creep screaming for help, burning up. Of course, the guards waited until the man had died before unlocking his cell. Ryder didn't blame them. The guards hated pedos as much as the prisoners did. The only thing worse than a pedo in prison was a rat.

In his second week at HELLview, he saw an old friend from his neighborhood, Jose. Jose was a big guy, 6ft 3 or so, and 240lbs, all muscle. He wasn't a one percenter, but everyone from the Iron Ravens Motorcycle club liked Jose. Jose was a great street fighter; in fact, he had never been beaten, from what Ryder remembered. Jose was standing in line at the chow hall when two small Mexican guys sneak attacked him and stabbed him to death. It had all happened so quickly. Prison politics dictated that Ryder could not step in and help his old friend, and he had to stand there helplessly as poor Jose bled to death. It was something no one deserved to ever witness, and it had left mental scars on Ryder.

The message to him was clear: no matter how big, no matter how strong, no matter how good a fighter you were, inside, it was truly survival of the fittest. On any given day, anyone could take you out. Walk up behind you and just shank you. Stay on high alert at all times and never truly trust anyone. It wasn't the guy who telegraphed his disdain to you who was the real threat, but the guy who was always smiling and claimed to be your friend. That was the guy to watch for. You let your guard down, and they take you out. He built a mental wall around himself to stay alive; that wall saved him on the inside, but once you had that wall, it was very hard to ever let anyone get close to you again. Lesson learned. D.T.A. Don't trust anyone.

CHAPTER 19

Coyote Ridge, Arizona.

Leanne Thorson had spent most of her life living in the town of Coyote Ridge, just 5 miles from Pine Hollow. Of Scandinavian stock, her Grandfather had been drawn to the Americas to seek fame and fortune as a miner. Apparently, he never made a red cent mining, but he and his brother had launched a general store right here in Coyote Ridge in the early 1900s that became the basis of the town.

When she was young, she loved the town and had an idyllic childhood, but by her teenage years, she was bored and restless. There was nothing to do after 6 pm in Coyote Ridge. The bright lights and excitement of the city of Phoenix called her name. She had managed to convince her parents to let her go to Phoenix to study. Leanne always had a passion for art and managed to get into Phoenix College, a distinguished art school.

Everything about Phoenix was amazing; it is such a big city and so spread out. There was every sort of restaurant you could imagine, all with world-class chefs. A vast array of bars and nightclubs, and endless events happening every day. She couldn't believe it. It was everything she wanted and more. She soon had a loyal circle of friends and a network of pals who knew what cool stuff was happening all over the Phoenix Metro every night of the week.

Her shared house just off Thomas Rd in midtown was so convenient that she could walk to school. Rent was affordable in Phoenix back in those days, too. From what Leanne heard, rents for a similar-sized house in Los Angeles or New York City would have been three times as much. They were crazy days, of course, this being before cell phones and social media, so they got away with blue murder.

Studying in the mornings, working in the afternoons and partying at night quickly caught up with Leanne. The first to go was studying. It was so much easier to sleep off the hangovers in the morning than drag your weary corpse to school to suffer in the classroom. Next to go was her art; she had always been creative, but who had time to sit and create every day when there were things to do? Leanne had started off as a waitress in a hipster restaurant to pay her way through school, but soon found that bartending in a dive bar paid a lot better. Plus, you basically got paid to drink, so that saved her money too. Getting paid to do what you love? Perfect!

At age 23, she met Brad, who worked in construction. They were like instant soul mates. Soon, she moved out of her shared house and moved in with Brad. He had his own house and was pretty much everything Leanne was looking for in a man. Tall, good-looking, loyal, funny and hard working, he checked off every box. By 25, she was pregnant and, at age 26, she was the mom to the best daughter ever, Tabitha.

After 4 years of raising Tabitha in Phoenix, they decided to move back to Coyote Ridge. Summers were cooler, land was cheaper, and it was just a better lifestyle for a young family with a daughter. They sold up Brad's house and managed to purchase a bigger house with a couple of acres just outside of town. Things were even better than life in Phoenix. Tabitha adjusted to her new life easily and had a small circle of friends, basically the children of Leanne's old friends from town.

On Tabitha's 11th birthday, they had promised to take her to her favorite restaurant in Flagstaff for a birthday dinner. Leanne had a terrible stomach bug and was bedridden, hunched over in pain. She told Tabitha they would need to postpone her birthday dinner until Leanne felt better, but Tabitha would not hear of it. She cried and threw herself around the house so much that finally Brad relented and told Leanne that he could take Tabitha to Flagstaff, and it could be a daddy/daughter dinner, and that mommy could take her out at a later date. Tabitha was good with that, and Leanne was in too much pain to argue.

They took off for Flagstaff at 4 pm, and Leanne took a nap. When she awoke, it was just after 10 pm. Had they come home when she slept? She got up and made her way to Tabitha's room. Perhaps Brad had come in, put her to bed and passed out on the couch? She checked her daughter's room, and nope, it was empty. Her bed had not been slept in. She checked the living room. Nothing. She went outside to look for Brad's truck, but it wasn't in the driveway. She was starting to worry now.

She called the restaurant in Flagstaff, but there was no answer. They had obviously closed for the night. Leanne started to panic; she called the local Sheriff's office, but there was no answer. She called the nearest emergency care place, but there was no sign of Brad and Tabitha. She contemplated driving to Flagstaff to see if she could find them, but she was still not feeling 100%. She called the number she had for the Flagstaff police station, but they were not helpful in the slightest. She must have passed back out on the couch around 5 am. Leanne was woken to someone thumping on the front door just after dawn that fateful morning.

She opened the door, and two cops stood there. All her worst nightmares were confirmed. There were only two reasons the cops showed up at your door so early in the morning! You were going to jail, or someone close to you just died. In her heart of hearts, she knew right away what they were here for.

She collapsed when they broke the news to her. A semi truck driver high on meth ran a red light and killed them both instantly. Her entire world was gone, in one cruel twist of fate. How? If there were a god, how could they let this happen? Her perfect world was wiped out in an instant. The police had to call emergency services and take her to the big hospital in Show Low. She was heavily medicated and held for 2 days. When Leanne was released, her sister Ingrid picked her up and drove her home. She was still in a daze; nothing seemed real. Ingrid and her husband, who was the Sheriff of Pine Hollow, had helped her prepare for the funerals.

For weeks after the tragedy, tears flowed. At times, Leanne thought she would never stop crying after the tears and the numbness came. Leanne thought she would never feel any sense of joy ever again. Besides, if she did, then who's to say that would not be taken away from her so cruelly as well? Some days, the sense of loss felt was just too much. She would lie in bed for days at a time with the curtains drawn, only getting up to hit the restroom and get a drink of water from the kitchen. She was not doing well.

Finally, Ingrid intervened – she and her husband had purchased the old Flanagan diner in Coyote Ridge, and Ingrid basically dragged herself out of bed to get her working behind the counter. Keeping busy was not a cure-all, but many times, with the breakfast and lunch time rush, there was little to no time to focus on the loss of her husband and only daughter.

Working twelve-hour shifts was enough of a distraction during the day to help her get back on her feet again and to stop thinking of her missing loved ones.

CHAPTER 20

Las Vegas, Nevada.

KC from the Dark Legion MC and his Bay Area boys found a decent diner near their motel in Las Vegas. One of his guys, Parrot head (named because he used to rock a bright red mohawk haircut), texted the Utah Dark Legion Chapter guys the address for the diner and instructed them to meet them there.

KC, Parrot head and Rhino ordered breakfast; their waitress was a young, fairly decent-looking 18 or 19-year-old. Rhino leered at her every time she passed their table, whispering inappropriate things under his breath. KC just laughed. *Boys will be boys, eh?*

Their waitress brought them their plates, and KC and his two club brothers tucked into their food with gusto. Screw waiting for the Utah guys. They can order their own food; it's not their fault that those boys were late.

"So what's the plan for the rest of the day?" asked Parrot Head.

"Well, we eat breakfast, wait for these Utah rubes to turn up, check out of our rooms and high tail it to Arizona. GPS tells me it will be about five or six hours, and then we waste this Steel Reaper prick." KC replied.

"Will there be a chance to stop for lunch along the way?" asked Rhino.

"Sure, we can hit a truck stop or even Flagstaff," KC replied. "Actually, let's hit Flagstaff, I've never been before, and I wanna check it out."

"Okay, cool, works for me," Rhino replied. "How far is Pine Hollow from Flagstaff?"

"I think a little over one hour," KC replied.

'Awesome," said Rhino

"Hey, how's your back today, prez?" asked Parrot Head between mouthfuls of bacon and egg.

"Yeah, pretty sore, man. I'm definitely out of practice on these long runs. As a club, we need to do more of them," said KC

"Yeah. I am the same. My shoulders are pretty sore, too," said Parrot Head. "I would definitely be down for more road trips, prez," he added.

"Well, that's cuz you got those stupid oversized ape hangers," said Rhino, "I keep telling ya, get some mini apes."

"Yeah, yeah," Parrot Head replied.

"Those big ape hangers are fine for cruising around town, but they wear you out on long hauls, brother," Rhino explained.

Just at that moment, the Utah boys finally arrived. Spotting KC and the Bay Area guys at the back of the diner, they hollered a loud AYOOO across the eating establishment. Every customer in the joint turned and looked at them. Some parents shook their heads and tsk-tsked.

Frank from Ogden, who was a semi-decent bodybuilder, squeezed in next to Rhino and Parrot head. "Move," he grunted as the two slid over in their booth.

Mike and Brendan from the Dark Legion's Utah chapter squeezed in next to KC, sitting opposite the others.

"Morning fellas," Frank greeted the Bay Area boys.

"Well, it's nearly afternoon now," stated Parrot Head.

"Whatever," Frank replied.

Mike studied his menu intensely. He was never one to turn down a good meal.

"How's the bacon here?" he asked.

"Yeah, pretty crispy," said Rhino, "Worth ordering."

"Ok, thanks," Mike replied.

'So what's the plan for today then?" asked Brendan.

'We check out, drive to Arizona, and you kill the Steel Reaper prick who shot Kyle," KC replied 'That's the plan."

"Good plan," said Brendan 'I like it."

"Me too," said Frank. 'Kyle must be avenged"

"Indeed," said KC," Although why you pricks didn't take him out down in Mexico I will never know."

"We told you," Mike bleated, "They had guns, we did not."

"Come on, man! A Dark Legion foot soldier doesn't let his brother get killed in front of his eyes, man, everyone knows that."

"Easier said than done," said Mike

"What did you say, Fatso?" snapped KC, "Don't ever contradict me like that again."

"Sorry, prez, just saying," said Mike, holding his head down.

"So what do we do after we kill this Steel Reaper? Get out of town?" asked Brendan.

"Yeah. Not too sure about the law enforcement situation in these small towns; it's probably just a local sheriff's department or something," said KC. "I say we do the job and get the hell out of dodge."

'Can we hit Phoenix?" asked Frank.

KC thought for a moment, "They might be thinking of that, probably best we high tail it to California soon as the dude is wasted."

"Ok, sounds good," said Brendan.

CHAPTER 21

Phoenix, Arizona.

Ryder packed his gear and checked his bike over to make sure nothing had rattled loose since he last rode it. After tightening a couple of bolts, he actually checked out the motel window, now expecting the motel car park to be swarming with cops looking for him after he assaulted their informant last night at the Filthy Hogg saloon. There seemed to be one crack head wandering around on the sidewalk just outside the motel property, but no army of cops with guns drawn, ready to take him out. Was the crack head an undercover cop? He thought for a moment and thought better of it. He recalled that, in the late 90s, he had seen undercover cops with fully tattooed arms, and he had never imagined that growing up. The thought of a skinny, emancipated police officer masquerading as a crack head seemed highly unlikely.

He wheeled his bike out through the front door of his motel room, did a quick dummy check of his room to make sure he had left nothing behind and then shut the door behind him. He went to the front office to return his key and once again, did a quick scout of the area to make sure there were no law enforcement types waiting to pounce on him. The coast seemed clear. Maybe he could get out of town without being arrested. He had to get to Northern Arizona and track down that rat Vince.

He fired up his scoot and rolled out of the motel car park. He headed north for a couple of blocks until he spied a Denny's. Dammit, he was hungry and in desperate need of some coffee, so he decided to pull over and grab breakfast. Everyone knew you can't go wrong with Denny's.

After eating, Ryder hit the gas station and topped up his tank. By his reckoning, it should take him approximately 3 hours to get to the town of Ironwood Bluff in Northern Arizona, even factoring in a gas station break to fill his tank. An easy day's riding. Ryder figured he would start in Ironwood Bluff, as it's the first small town after Show Low, and work his way North, hitting each town on that stretch of highway, which meant Coyote Ridge and Pine Hollow to track down Vince. He could almost taste the vengeance now; it had only been 25 years in the making.

The ride out of the Phoenix metro area was smooth sailing. Ryder was surprised by how much Phoenix had grown since he last visited. In an alternative timeline of his life, he could see himself living in Arizona rather than California. California's once progressive policies had put the state above most of the nation; now, these policies had pretty much ruined the state.

Arizona seemed much more like the California of the 80s, where people do what they want to do. Want to wear a helmet? Sure! Don't want to wear one? That's cool too. Want an electric vehicle? Sure, knock yourself out, you do you. Don't want one? That's cool too. Crazy how the government in California now dictates every aspect of its residents' lives. It felt like living in Communist Russia these days. Maybe Ryder would move after this was all done anyway.

90 minutes into his ride, he found a gas station and pulled over. He gassed up and went inside to get a soda and some munchies. It

felt good to walk around a bit and get his legs moving again. He was still out of practice on these long rides. In the old days, he could do 12 hours without issue. He could see why a lot of the old timers had switched out from hard tail choppers to Road Kings, it was like cruising down the highway in a La-Zee-Boy chair. Pure comfort.

After resting up for 15 minutes, Ryder continued his ride to the North East. Soon, he saw the signs for Show Low and knew it wouldn't be long now. He planned to check into a local motel in each town and spend a few days there, getting to know some of the locals, hit each bar in town and start fact-finding. Sooner or later, he would come across someone who knew of Vince and where he was hiding out.

After passing through Show Low, Ryder soon saw signs for the town of Ironwood Bluff. That would be the first stop for him. Cruise into town, find a motel, check in and get to explore. He was confident Vince was somewhere in this part of the world. Had the scum bag changed his name? Had he drastically changed his appearance? Ryder didn't know, but in his heart, something told him there would be a way to track him down. He owed this. 20 years of his life lost to his so-called "brother". His youth is gone, all for a few dollars.

Ryder pulled off the highway and took the road into Ironwood Bluff, a decent-sized mountain town with a main street that ran about 5 blocks and suburban houses set back a few blocks on either side of the commercial district. Ryder could just see Vince arriving here 20 years ago with bags of money (his money!), buying up an affordable property, and reinventing himself. He had to be here; he could feel it.

Ryder cruised down the busy shopping district, scanning the various stores. So far, he had spotted a couple of restaurants, 2 pawn shops, a supermarket and a bunch of bars. He saw two locals standing in front of a hardware store and decided to pull up and see if they could recommend a motel for him.

Ryder assumed these two nice old geezers had never lived anywhere else in their lives but Ironwood Bluff. Perhaps they instinctively knew the rest of the world would never be as good, so why bother leaving and finding out, eventually, that you were right? Fair enough.

They seemed helpful enough and recommended a small motel just past the end of First Avenue (Which was what Main Street was called in this town). In Ryder's experience, pulling into small towns with a loud motorcycle, a leather jacket and a bad attitude, most locals were not going to be your friend. Perhaps because he was now older and wiser, or perhaps he wasn't riding with a horde of other bikers, but these two were friendly and non-judgmental. Made a nice change.

Ryder found the motel with ease. The old geezer's directions were spot on. That was definitely a handy travel tip: ask the locals for directions. Ryder booked a room for 4 nights, figuring drinking in each bar in town once would clue him up to any intel on that rat Vince. He had counted 5 bars, but he figured he could always bounce to the next one if one was dead. He would spend his days networking with local restaurants and stores and fishing for intel from them, too. Someone would know Vince. They had to. It wasn't like major cities like Chicago or New York City, where there were so many new faces arriving daily and everyone minded their own business.

The motel seemed clean and safe, despite having décor right out of the 1970s, but still Ryder decided to wheel his motorcycle indoors just to be sure. He didn't have the money to replace his bike if it got stolen or damaged. After checking in and dumping his gear, he decided to take a walk back up First Avenue and grab some food. He needed to stretch his legs, and despite snacking earlier, he could do with a proper meal before he started hitting the bars. He walked back into town, saying hello or good day to every local that he passed. One or two looked straight past him, but most returned the greeting.

He stopped into the local pawn shop that he had seen on his way into town and checked out what they had on sale. He admired a couple of good-quality used guitars. Ryder figured if he ever got a do-over for this life, he would have put time and energy into learning a musical instrument, probably the guitar, then a life of crime. He liked the idea of getting up, playing music and entertaining other people. The cards had not gone that way for him in life, so it was more of a pipe dream than anything else.

Ryder examined the gun section. Even in a small mountain town in Arizona, they had a better range of weapons than the average Californian gun store. Another reason the state of Arizona was growing on him. Ryder had contemplated buying a weapon to decimate Vince, but with his criminal record, a background check was out of the question. He didn't have a reliable connection on the black market to purchase a weapon and didn't trust meeting a guy in a dive bar. His rule of thumb after years of living with criminals had become: If a guy in a bar approaches you about anything illegal, there's a good chance he was an undercover cop or a paid informant. He had not come this far to find his ass ending up back in the California Prison system. No thanks.

He contemplated picking up a good used Shotgun. Affordable and reliable, the biggest drawback was their size. Hard to conceal on your person. He remembered when he had first joined the Iron Ravens; some of the older guard did prefer shotguns, but they usually sawed off the majority of the barrel and half the stock so they could hide them under their jackets. Perhaps he could do that.

He saw it. It was like a custom-made sawn-off shotgun. The handle was weird, but it seemed like the perfect size. What the hell was that? They never sold these back in his day. He was curious. He looked around for the Pawn Shop worker.

The man saw that Ryder was looking for him and approached.

"Can I help you with anything, son?" asked the elderly owner.

'You sure can. What's that there?" Ryder asked.

"Oh, that's a Mossberg 500 Shockwave," the elderly man smiled.

'That's legal?" asked Ryder.

"Certainly is," the store owner replied, "Because it's not a shoulder-fired weapon, it doesn't classify as a shotgun. Actually, technically it's neither a shotgun nor a handgun."

'Wow, they never had those back in my day," said Ryder 'Can I check it out?"

The store owner unlocked the case and retrieved the weapon for Ryder.

"You've been out of the country or something for the last 20 years," the owner asked before handing Ryder the weapon.

'Yeah, uh, Europe. I was living in Europe with my wife. Now I am divorced and back in Arizona," Ryder lied, thinking fast.

Ryder checked out the weapon, pumped it, and tested the action.

"So I assume there is a fair bit of kick on one of these?" Ryder asked.

"Yeah, somewhat. I wouldn't recommend it to an inexperienced shooter," said the old timer. "They're great for home defense, by the way."

'I can see that," said Ryder, smiling. He didn't want to admit it, but he really did like the weapon. How could he purchase it legally, though? Maybe he could come back at night and steal it. He nixed that idea right away, as it would be obvious now to the old man who the thief was.

Ryder handed the Mossberg back to the owner. Thanks, I'll be back in a few days to pick it up," he explained.

"No problem, young man, you know where to find me," said the owner before locking it back up.

Ryder left the store determined to own that firearm before he left town.

CHAPTER 22

Pine Hollow, Arizona.

Joe paced back and forth. He couldn't stand still. He felt sick, his stomach cramped. *Is this it? Is this how I go out? Shot dead in a field by a bunch of young punks?* Adrenaline surged through his body. He tried to control himself, but his knees were shaking. *I can't let anyone see me like this,* he thought.

He had to get it together. He had been through a lot in life, some truly terrifying situations, but one of the few reasons he had made it this far was that he didn't let fear get the best of him. Why was he doing so now? If he was going to survive this, he had to show strength. He had to get his head right. He had to face them man to man and somehow convince them not to kill him. Was it possible?

Joe never killed that Dark Legions kid. Johnny did. Was his whole plan based on them confronting him, him telling them, "Hey, it wasn't me, it was this guy," and then them saying 'Well, okay then, no problem, have a good day, sir, we shall be on our way now"?

Who was he fooling? Even if they accepted that, their pride would demand a victim, and he would be that person. The guys they had drunk with in that small diner back in Mexico were a good twenty years younger than Joe and Johnny, but he was confident in a one-on-one fight; he could probably hold his own against one of them.

Maybe two of them if they didn't know how to fight? Any more than that, he was in for a kicking.

Joe thought back to the knights of old and how a champion would be selected to defend the Queen's honor if the King was too feeble to fight. Joe was hoping he could have the Dark Legion guys select 1 "Champion" to fight him. Appeal to their warped sense of honor. Fist on Fist, no weapons. Fight like men. Sure, he might lose a few teeth and get a bloodied nose or something, but that was better than the entire club peppering him full of lead. That had to be his best chance.

Joe looked down. He was wearing out the grass under his feet, pacing back and forth so much. He was still in panic mode. He had a somewhat decent plan now and was still shaking. He recalled an ex-girlfriend of his, who got into all this spiritual crap and ended up taking off to Sedona to teach yoga. She was a big believer in meditation and tried to teach him. Joe looked around and found a nice spot deep into the lush, overgrown grass. He sat down and tried to remember her lessons. Breathe in through the nose, hold it and breathe out through the mouth. Clear your mind and focus on the inhale/hold/exhale.

He sat down in the grass and tried to cross his legs. He was too stiff and seized up to cross them properly like you did as a kid, but he tried his best. What should he do with his hands? He tried to sit like a yogi Buddha, or someone. He closed his eyes and tried to concentrate on his breathing. He felt stupid. This is stupid, he thought. If they pulled up to me now, they would probably die laughing. *Maybe that wasn't a bad thing.*

He was thinking about "stuff" and not focusing on his breathing. He tried to clear his mind and just focus on a deep breath in through the nose, hold it and then exhale through his mouth. He wondered what Stacy was doing in Sedona. *Did she miss him?* Shit, he wasn't focusing on his breathing again. He cleared his mind again and focused on his breath.

The sun was setting, and he could feel it shining on his face. The air was clear here. There was a quiet here that he had never experienced living in Phoenix. There was always background noise during the day, living in Phoenix. He could hear a couple of birds chirping in the distance, but that was it. Even that was relaxing. He continued to clear his mind and just focus on breathing.

Joe opened his eyes. He wasn't sure how long he had been out for, but he felt completely different. Maybe there was something to this meditation BS after all? He felt different. Something told him that somehow he would get through this. He would survive. He wasn't sure how or why, considering he killed his best friend, but now he felt it was all going to be okay. He stood up and wiped his ass and the back of his jeans to get sticks and grass off his pants. He shook his legs and arms out and limbered up. Bring it on. Do your worst. It's gonna be okay.

He walked back towards the car park area. Looking up, he saw 3 carloads of people approaching. Is this it? They're here already? Oh well, better bring what you got, cuz Joe was not going to go down without a fight.

CHAPTER 23

Ironwood Bluff, Arizona.

Ryder ate dinner and then hit the first bar he came across. After sitting at the bar for an hour, people started talking to him as they came up and ordered drinks right by him. Some were a little apprehensive seeing a new face in town, but after a few drinks, they would shoot the shit with him. He ended up having an in-depth conversation with two old timers, and feeling confident, he pulled out a photo of him and Vince from 25 years ago.

He explained he was looking for his long-lost friend Vince, and the last he had heard, Vince was living up in these parts. After studying the photo for a few moments, one of the old geezers said he had never seen Vince before, and the other was convinced it was Old Man Stewart. Ryder tried to casually ask about Old Man Stewart, but the possibility of him being Vince seemed slim to none. The man they were talking about had lived in town for over 50 years. Despite the facts, Ryder figured he would try to check out this guy regardless, just in case it was Vince. Memory is a funny thing. Perhaps Vince did arrive here 25 years ago, and in their minds, it had been 50 years. We would never be able to tell unless he met Old Man Stewart.

After buying the old boys' whiskey shots, they explained that Old Man Stewart ran the plumbing service in town. Ryder would figure out in the morning where this was and "swing by". After one more beer, he paid his bar tab and walked back to his motel. Not a bad first night; he had one potential lead to check out.

The next morning, he ate breakfast and asked at the family-run diner where the plumber's store was. Turns out it was an old suburban house converted into a work premises, which is why Ryder hadn't spotted it riding into town. He paid up for his breakfast and wandered down the side streets trying to find Old Man Stewart's place. He was just turning the corner, wondering where the hell this place was, when he saw an old geezer loading up a work truck. Could this be him? Maybe it was Old Man Stewart's father or something?

The man noticed him walking towards the work truck.

"Morning, beautiful day," the old Geezer said.

'Sure is," said Ryder. "I'm looking for Old Man Stewart," Ryder explained.

"That would be me," the old Geezer replied.

"Ah, very cool. I was drinking in a bar in town last night, and two men recommended your plumbing service."

The old geezer chuckled 'That would be Bobby and Frankie."

'Yeah, that's them," Ryder replied.

"I haven't seen you before. Are you new in town?" asked Old Man Stewart.

Ryder thought fast 'Ah, no, I live in Coyote Ridge. I was wondering if you work in my town," Ryder explained.

Old Man Stewart thought for a moment, "New Jersey Hank not working out for you?

Ryder figured Hank must be the local plumber in Coyote Ridge. "Eh, just, well, you know," Ryder replied, shrugging his shoulders.

"Yeah, I figured as much. He was always a poor workman. Cutting corners and charging double," grizzled old man Stewart.

"That would be him," said Ryder, shaking his head, making out he was exasperated by New Jersey Hank's service.

"Well, do you need doing, son?" asked the old man.

"I just need some pipes replaced in my bathroom," lied Ryder.

Old Man Stewart wiped his brow and shook his head. 'To be honest with you, son, Ironwood keeps me pretty busy. I wouldn't even be able to come over and check it out for at least two weeks."

"Oh, I see," Ryder replied. He did not need to continue this conversation; it was quite apparent that this was not Vince.

The old man stood there staring blankly at Ryder.

'Well, do you have a business card or something? Perhaps I can call you in a couple of weeks and check your availability then," said Ryder.

"I certainly do," said Old Man Stewart, fishing into his overall pocket 'Here you go."

"Thanks," said Ryder, accepting the card and pretending to study it.

'What did you say your name was?" asked the old Geezer.

"Josh," lied Ryder, "Josh Jones"

"Ahh, a JJ, very cool. I'll remember that for when you call me," said the old man. "Nice meeting you and all the best"

"Thanks, you too," said Ryder, turning and walking back towards the main part of town.

That night Ryder hit two bars. One was dead, he had two drinks, left there and hit the next. It was a younger crowd, and people kept to themselves. Whenever he tried to have a conversation, the person just stared blankly at him and walked away. First off, very rude.

How Ryder was raised if someone spoke to you, Ryder was raised to reply. Secondly, it became apparent to him that this town was turning out to be a dead end. Perhaps he should check out of his motel tomorrow morning and head to the next town over, Coyote Ridge.

Ryder woke the next morning and decided it was time to move on. If the rest of the towns in this area didn't come to fruition, he could always come back again, but somewhere, his gut instinct told him Ironwood Bluff was a dead end. He loaded up his bike and rolled it out of his motel room. Ryder went to the front office to return his key card and pay his tab.

After that, he fired up his Harley and let it idle for a minute while he contemplated his next move. Examining Old Man Stewart's business card in his wallet, he came across the Arizona driver's license for the informant he had bashed at the Filthy Hogg a couple of days ago. The driver's license photo kind of looked like a younger version of him. He wanted that Mossberg 500 Shockwave. Ryder made up his mind. He would head back to that pawn shop and try to purchase that weapon.

He rode his bike down First Avenue searching for the pawn shop. When he arrived, it hadn't opened yet. He checked his phone. 15 minutes to opening time. He sat on his bike and waited. 5 minutes later, Ryder spotted the owner walking up First Ave. He was on time. When the old store owner recognized Ryder, he gave him a little wave. *Oh, good, he remembers me,* thought Ryder. Ryder waited until the old geezer unlocked the door and switched on all the lights. He left his helmet on his bike and went inside.

"You've come for that Mossberg, I see," said the old timer.

"Yes, thanks, it's too good to say no to," Ryder explained.

The old man grabbed a set of keys and went to the gun cabinet to unlock it. He retrieved the Mossberg 500 Shockwave and returned to the front counter.

"You want ammo with that, son?" he asked Ryder.

"Sure. A box of shells would be great," Ryder replied. The thought of using an informant's cash to purchase a weapon to kill Vince tickled Ryder.

'I need ID," said the old man. Ryder carefully extracted JC's license from his wallet. It wouldn't do him any good to pull out two driver's licenses at once.

The old geezer examined the license and eyed Ryder. 'Wow, barely recognize you with that big bushy beard," the old man exclaimed.

"Yeah, old photo," shrugged Ryder.

'I can see that. Clearly, it's you, though – I can tell by the eyes and the nose," the old man replied.

"Of course," Ryder smiled lamely.

"Jean Claude Thomson?" asked the old man.

"Yeah, my mother was French and my father was Irish," Ryder lied.

The old man filled out some paperwork, Ryder signed it and gave the guy the cash. After the transaction was finished, Ryder stuffed the weapon and shells into his backpack and said his goodbyes. He highly doubted he would ever come back to the town of Ironwood Bluff.

CHAPTER 24

Pine Hollow, Arizona.

Joe tensed up as he saw the three cars approaching him, not out of fear but in determination to stand his ground. The cars slowed and came to a stop in the "car park" section of the field. He cautiously walked closer to them. Expecting bikers in leather jackets with club vests emblazoned with patches, he was quite surprised to see a bunch of high schoolers exit the three vehicles. High school kids? Do they realize they could be in the middle of a gunfight?

Would the Sheriff hold him responsible if someone copped a bullet? Fuck he didn't need this. Somehow, he would be blamed.

As he approached the car park area, he realized most of these kids looked familiar to him. These high school kids were local. Joe walked closer.

"You shouldn't be here," he shouted over to the ones nearest to him.

"And why's that?" asked a preppy-looking guy. Joe guessed he was 18, maybe 19.

"Cuz shit's about to kick off here, that's why," Joe explained.

"Yeah, we know. That's why we are here," the preppy kid replied.

Joe looked at him. This kid was familiar to Joe.

"Hey, do I know you? Asked Joe.

The kid stared at Joe. "Nah, don't think so."

Joe thought for a moment. He did know this kid; he was the town's lawyer's son. "You're Ben Fine's son, ain't ya?"

The kid looked somewhat surprised. *Joe did know him.* "Yeah, I'm Richard," he finally responded.

"Yeah, I thought you looked familiar. Look, man, you can't be here. Shit's about to go down, and Sheriff Williams ain't gonna be happy if you and your friends are here."

Richard stood there defiantly. "Hey man, it's a free world. We can do what we want."

'Yeah, fair enough. But some guys are coming here in the next hour to "kick my ass". If you kids get hurt in the process, Sheriff Williams is gonna blame me," said Joe, his patience wearing thin.

"Sheriff Williams can suck it," Richard replied 'He can't make us leave if we don't want to. If he does, my dad will sue his ass."

Oh great, just what I needed to day groaned Joe in his head. *Some jumped-up lawyer's kid threatening lawsuits if he doesn't get his own way.*

"Well, if ya get shot, just remember I did try and warn ya," said Joe.

"We'll be fine, buddy," Richard shouted back, helping his friends unload picnic blankets and coolers (of which Joe assumed were beers and white claws"

One of the kids cranked up a car stereo. Jelly Roll was playing.

Damn, these kids think this is some kind of party fumed Joe. He ran through his options in his head. Chase them away? Somehow, the Sheriff would blame him. Maybe it was best they were here?

They could be witnesses. Might keep some of those Dark Legion scumbags from fighting dirty or just gunning him down in cold blood. Try to see it as an advantage and not a disadvantage, perhaps?

One of the girls in the convoy came down to Joe and offered him a white claw. He didn't drink that stuff. Plus, he wanted to keep a clear head before the Dark Legion turned up.

'Want a drink, mister?" she asked, extending a cold alcoholic beverage to him.

"No thanks," he replied.

'We all thought you would just skip town," she exclaimed.

'Why would I do that? I've done nothing wrong," Joe replied.

'Won't they kill you if they find you here?" she asked.

"Well, what choice do I have? I run, and they will chase me. One day you just have to stand your ground, you know?'

The high schooler thought for a moment. "Yeah, I didn't think about that. I guess you're right."

"Like I said, I did nothing wrong. Running just makes you appear guilty," Joe replied.

"So you're not worried about dying then?" she asked Joe.

"Of course I am, but you know what? Any of us could die any day. You might cross the street going to school and get hit by a drunk driver. None of us knows how much time we have left on this planet. We just gotta do the best we can with what we are given, ya know?" said Joe.

"Not me, I'm going to live forever," said the High School girl. "By the time I get old, they will figure out a way to keep us all alive."

"I doubt it, but okay. Just try and stay out of the way when these guys arrive, okay?" asked Joe.

The girl looked at him like he had just taken a shit in his own hand and tried to shake hers. "Well, yeah. Okay," with that, she walked off.

Kids today fumed Joe, shaking his head.

CHAPTER 25

Northern Arizona.

KC rode up front as his Dark Legions followed in rank. He saw the turn-off signs for Flagstaff and gave his brothers the signal. The followed him to the exit ramp and stayed in formation like a well-trained group of fighter pilots.

They cruised North on the I-17 until KC spotted a sign for Denny's near the Northern Arizona University Campus. That would do, you couldn't go wrong with Denny's. KC waved again, and like a well-oiled machine, the rest of the club slowed and pulled into the restaurant car park.

KC chose a parking spot that the windows could see of the diner, and he and the boys took over 2 spots, fitting 3 bikes in each. No chance of some dumbass civilian pulling in and knocking down their bikes with 3 in each spot. He had seen people bashed for knocking over a Dark Legion rider's bike, and rightfully so. Most people just didn't "see" motorcycles when they were on the road or looking for a parking spot.

He waited until everyone had shut down their Harleys before heading in. It was between lunch and the dinner rush now, so the restaurant was fairly empty, and they managed to take over a large booth overlooking their bikes.

The boys looked through the menus, trying to figure out what they wanted to eat. KC decided on a burger and fries, and everyone else followed suit, but Frank ordered a grilled chicken salad.

Half the guys ordered beers, but KC decided to order a Coke as he wanted to keep a clear head until the Steel Reaper prick was pushing up daisies. Then he would celebrate.

The waitress brought over their lunch orders. It was easy to figure out since only Frank ordered something different. The brothers quickly passed the plates down the table until everyone had an order.

Mike, the chubbiest guy in the club, announced loudly 'Which faggot ordered a salad?"

A man eating a late lunch with his family, a couple of tables up, "Tsk'd," loudly.

Mike looked up and gave the father a filthy look. The man quickly looked down.

"I did," said Frank 'Perhaps you should get one as well, ya fatty."

"Well fuck you, Frank," said Mike rather loudly. The father, two booths up, said something under his breath that they had all heard. Mike again stared at the man, if looks could kill. "Besides, I'm not fat, I'm just big boned."

"Yeah, okay, there, Eric Cartman," quipped Parrot Head.

'Fuck off," Mike replied. Again, the father, two booths up from the bikers, said something under his breath that none of the one percenters clearly heard.

Everyone tucked into their food at top speed, like their lives depended on it. After Mike had cleared his plate, he started picking fries off everyone else's plates, too. "You finished with that?" 'You want that last fry?' he would ask as he took them from the other guy's plates.

They had finished eating, and KC contemplated getting some coffee to round out their meal. At that moment, Mike let out an overly loud belch, which had half the restaurant turning around and looking at them.

"Sign of a good meal," he proudly announced.

"Oh fer gawd's sake," the father two booths up exclaimed. That was it, Mike pushed Frank out of the way and got up from their booth. He stormed over to the family man sitting two booths up.

'You got a problem faggot?" Mike raged

'Look, I am trying to have lunch with my kids," the man replied 'Why do you have to curse like that?"

"I don't need to curb my behavior for you, asshole," raged Mike.

'Do you mind?" the father of two said to Mike.

'Yeah, I mind," said Mike, grabbed the man by the scruff of his shirt and dragged him out of the booth. The man pushed and pulled against Mike, but it was clear that he did not have any fight training whatsoever.

KC, seeing where this was heading, nodded at the boys and urged them to get up.

'C'mon," he said, getting up and out of the booth. He approached his club brother. Mike was not always right in the way he handled things with the general public, but at the end of the day, he was a brother, and KC had to support him. The rest of the guys followed suit.

The man's wife started screaming and crying. That set his two daughters off, and now the whole restaurant was looking at them.

By now, Rhino, Parrot Head, Frank and Brendan were by KC's side. The manager, witnessing what happened, urged the line cooks to follow him out from behind the counter. The two cooks both had meat cleavers in their hands. KC seemed to be the only one of his boys who noticed.

"Hey, hey," shouted the manager, "Let him go."

Mike finally noticed the two armed cooks. He released the man's collar from his grip.

"Outside, you guys, we will have no violence in my restaurant," shouted the manager.

Mike contemplated attacking the manager but thought better of it. Reluctantly, the bikers filed outside.

The manager and the two cooks stood behind the front doors, watching them leave.

"Hey, how about that, fellas," said Mike, very proud of himself. "Don't all thank me at once. But, we just scored ourselves a free meal."

Parrot head patted him on the back 'Good job, fella," he laughed. The bikers grabbed their Harleys and one by one fired them up. KC always loved the sound of an idling Harley, no idea why.

"Alright, boys," he announced 'Who's ready to go kill a Steel Reaper?"

The men all cheered. One by one, they rolled out of the Denny's car park on their way to the town of Pine Hollow.

CHAPTER 26

Ironwood Bluff, Arizona.

Satisfied with his purchase of the Mossberg, Ryder rolled out of the town of Ironwood Bluff. He might have wasted a few days here searching for his once friend and now sworn enemy, Vince, but at least it wasn't an entire waste. He had managed to legally (well, kinda) purchase a sweet little shotgun, or was it a pistol? What did it matter? He was coming for Vince, and nothing was going to stop him now.

He rolled North on Highway 77 towards the town of Coyote Ridge. By the looks of his paper map, which he had studied before checking out of the motel, it shouldn't take him more than 15 minutes to get there. He was enjoying the ride. Ryder could barely believe he was still in Arizona. He felt like he was in Colorado, Switzerland or somewhere deep in Europe.

Before too long, Ryder saw the signs for the turn off to the town of Coyote Ridge. He was almost disappointed in a sense, as he could have done a two-to-three-hour ride versus a 12-minute ride. Oh well, he wasn't in this part of the country for a pleasure ride; he was here for business. The business of revenge.

Just as in the case of Ironwood Bluff, Ryder cruised slowly through the town of Coyote Ridge before turning around and cruising back the way he had come just to get the feel for the place.

Then he rode back to the West side of town to a small motel he had spotted on his first run through. Much like the town of Ironwood Bluff, Coyote Ridge had a small main street with a handful of diners, bars, gift shops and other random small businesses. He would repeat the process he had started back in Ironwood, leave the scoot in his motel room, get to know the locals and fish for information.

After checking into the local motel, Ryder rolled through the car park towards his room. He parked his scooter out front, unlocked the door and went inside. It wasn't the Ritz, but it wasn't the worst place he had stayed in either. He recalled staying in a motel just outside of Baltimore in his early 20s. They found a knife under the mattress, and the bathroom looked like someone had been murdered there, and the room had been poorly cleaned up. Brown stains are all over the walls. He had stayed one night, barely slept and checked out the next day. Never again.

Then again, even that shit hole was better than some of the cells he had been put in during his life behind bars. Your own private bathroom? A win! Not being able to hear grown men crying or screaming at night? A win! Being able to walk to the local store and buy whatever food and drink you want and eat it in your motel room? Another win. That was one good thing about surviving the Californian prison system. After that, every place you stayed seemed like a palace in comparison.

Ryder dumped his backpack and helmet on the well-worn bed. He retrieved the Mossberg and shells and tucked it under the bed. No sense in a nosey maid or motel clerk finding it. After hiding the weapon, he went back and retrieved his bike. Coyote Ridge seemed like a nice, quiet mountain town with a low crime rate, but why leave his bike out and tempt the local criminal element?

He rolled it in. Satisfied it would be safe in the room, he locked up and strolled back into the town.

He walked up the town's Main Street, nodded and greeted all the locals as he strode up the sidewalk. *Seemed like an idyllic place to raise a family,* thought Ryder, especially in this day and age. Who would try to raise a family in a big city like New York or Los Angeles these days? Way too much crime and drug zombies. A small place like this was almost like rolling the clock back to the 1950s. Leave it to Beaver. Simpler times. He could see the appeal.

He saw a pawn shop. Almost out of habit, he decided to go in and check it out despite the fact that he already had a weapon. Old habits die hard, he guessed.

The old boy behind the counter greeted him when he walked in. Ryder said hello back and browsed the store. They had a couple of decent rifles, but nothing cool or interesting enough for him to get his wallet out of his pocket for. It then occurred to him that he had yet to eat today. He needed to find a nice, quiet diner and get some breakfast into him. He said goodbye to the Pawn Shop owner and headed up the street in search of a good spot to eat. One block up the street, he saw a sign "Flanagans Family Diner," that looked promising.

Ryder reached the diner and peered into the window. It looked like it was right out of the 1950s. Some photographers could have easily staged a "Life in the 1950s" photo shoot inside the premises, and no one would believe it was shot in 2025.

Looks perfect thought Ryder as he pulled the door open to enter the restaurant. *Hopefully, the food will be of an old-fashioned style too.*

The diner was busy, so Ryder found himself seated at the front counter. Usually, he would prefer not to eat with his back exposed to strangers (old habits die hard), but after quickly scoping out everyone in the busy restaurant, he felt confident enough that there were no imminent threats behind him.

The waitress had her back to him when Ryder sat down, apparently deep in conversation with one of the line cooks. He was in no hurry; *let her take her time*, he thought. She finished her conversation and turned to face the counter. She stopped mid-spin. Ryder was stunned; it was the woman from his recurring dreams in prison. How? Why? What was going on? She was apparently just as shocked as he was.

She stopped and stared at him before regaining her composure.

"Heyyy, Hi, uh, sorry, didn't see you there," she said.

'Well, you were deep in conversation by the looks of things," Ryder replied.

"Uh, yeah. Yeah, I was," the woman blushed. "I'm sorry, I feel like I know you from somewhere."

'America's Most Wanted, probably," joked Ryder.

'Ha ha you're funny. Let me get you a menu," said the woman.

'Thanks," said Ryder.

"You know what you want to drink?" asked the woman 'Coffee? Tea?"

"Coffee, thanks," Ryder replied, still skimming over the menu.

"You know what you want, or do you need a few more minutes, hon?" asked the lady.

Ryder fought the urge to reply 'I want you," and instead said, "Yeah, give me the breakfast special, with bacon, whole wheat toast and grape jelly."

"How do you want your eggs?" she asked.

"Oh, scrambled," Ryder replied, handing her back the menu.

She returned with coffee and a glass of iced water.

"So you're going to tell me?" she asked.

"Uh, tell you what?" asked Ryder.

'Where have we met? I'm terrible with names but good with faces. It's great, in fact. Where and when did we meet?" she asked.

"I'm telling you we have never met before," Ryder replied.

"We definitely have," the woman replied.

'I really don't think we have," Ryder replied. "Oh, I'm Ryder, by the way. R, Y, D, E, R, not R, I, D, E, R"

The woman extended her hand, "Hi Ryder, with a Y. I am Leanne, L, E, A, N, N, E," she explained.

'Nice to meet you, Leanne. You own this place? Does that make you, Leanne Flanagan?" Ryder asked.

'Nah, my sister and her husband own it," Leanne replied, "I'm the manager."

'So they're the Flanagans?" he asked.

"Williams, actually. The Flanagans were the previous owners and founders, and we just kept the name as it's tradition in this town."

"Very cool," said Ryder, nodding in appreciation.

Leanne took care of some customers as Ryder consumed his tasty breakfast. He could tell right away these were real eggs, not that powdered or liquid crap that so many chain restaurants try to pass off as eggs these days. Ryder made a mental note to come back here tomorrow as well.

By the time he had cleared his plate of food, the restaurant was thinning out from the morning's customers. Leanne and a waitress were collecting plates and wiping down the tables. After taking a tray of plates into the kitchen, she returned with the coffee pot to Ryder's section of the counter.

"More coffee, Ryder with a Y?" she asked.

'Sure, thanks," he said, holding out his cup for a refill.

She returned the coffee pot and came back with her own cup of Joe.

'So you're the guy that bought the Harrison house up on the hill, eh?" she asked him.

'Harrison? What? Oh no, not me," Ryder replied.

"On vacation?" Leanne asked.

"Actually, I'm looking for a long-lost friend," said Ryder.

"Oh, that's so cool," said Leanne, "You got a photo of him or something? If he lives in this town, chances are I'll know him."

Ryder grabbed his wallet and fished out a picture of him and Vince from 25 years ago and handed it to Leanne.

'Yeah, that guy looks familiar," she said

Ryder peered down at the picture. "No, that's me," he explained.

"Wow, that's you? You've changed a lot," she exclaimed.

"Well, we all get older," shrugged Ryder.

"No, no, you look great, trust me," said Leanne, "You just look so different."

"Well, shaving your head and growing a beard will do that, I guess," said Ryder. 'It's the other guy."

Leanne studied the photo. "When was this taken?" she asked.

"Oh, about 25 years ago, right before he moved to Northern Arizona," said Ryder.

"Hmm," thought Leanne, "I might have still been living in Phoenix then."

"Oh well, worth a shot," said Ryder, taking the photo back from her and carefully putting it back in his wallet.

"Any more coffee?" asked Leanne.

"Heck no," Ryder replied 'If I have any more, I am going to be bouncing off the walls."

Leanne laughed at that.

"Say, what are you doing after this?" asked Leanne.

"Nothing planned, but I might need to take a stroll around town to walk this meal off," Ryder replied.

"Well, if you can wait around for 30 minutes, I would be happy to serve as your tour guide," suggested Leanne.

Ryder thought for a second. *Was she into him or just being nice?* It had been so long since he had spent any significant time with women that he was out of practice understanding their cues.

"Sure, that would be cool," he said, playing it off nonchalantly.

Leanne beamed from ear to ear. "Ok, I won't be long, I promise," she said, disappearing back into the kitchen.

Ryder sat and sipped on his coffee. He was ready to cut and run to the next town over, the one called Pine Hollow, but told himself a few more days here in Coyote Ridge couldn't possibly hurt. She did say there were a few years when she was in Phoenix. Perhaps Vince had arrived then and assimilated into town under another name? It was worth sticking around, just to be sure. The company of a beautiful woman? A nice surprise and an added bonus.

True to her word, Leanne was ready and finished in 30 minutes. She gave instructions to the waitress and promised the young woman she would be back at 5 pm before the dinner rush started, and escorted Ryder out of Flanagan's fine dining establishment.

Her insider's guide to the town of Coyote Ridge took all of 30 minutes. After giving him a quick rundown of all the stores and who was who in town, she led him to a picturesque overlook with a massive green valley below. After years of being held in by large concrete walls, the view over the pines took Ryder's breath away. He never really had an appreciation for nature until it was taken away from him. He guessed the old saying was true 'You don't know what you've got till it's gone."

In all his years inside, Ryder never got to see the stars. Now, he made sure to always look up at the night sky and take in what he had lost for over 20 years. Out here, in Northern Arizona, there was far less "Light pollution" than in California or the city of Phoenix, and the number of stars he could see at night was mind-blowing. Growing up, he was taught that by the year 2020, we would be taking holidays on the moon. None of that ever happened, but he still couldn't help stare in wonder at the power of the universe.

Leanne directed him to a nice shady spot, and they sat on the grass and talked about life. To Ryder's surprise, Leanne leaned in and kissed him. He returned the kiss. Had women changed this much in 25 years, or did he just miss the cues to make the first move on her? Either way, he was happy she put herself out there like that, as he, too, had wanted to kiss her. Dammit, being locked up so long had made him way out of practice on what to do with women.

They made out for a while, and then Leanne told Ryder she had to get back for the evening shift. She explained to him that she would be finished by 9 pm and could meet him for a drink if he wanted. He agreed and walked with her back to Flanagans. After seeing her off, he decided to head back to his hotel, shower and take a quick power nap.

Ryder pounded some coffee after he woke from his power nap. He used the little coffee maker supplied in his room. He knew it wasn't the best coffee on the market, but it was free and in his room, saving him from heading down the street to purchase some. Apparently, power naps were meant to be good for you, but he always felt like dog shit after waking up from one. What are ya gonna do?

He left his motel around 8 pm, walking down the now pretty much deserted Main Street. Everyone was at home on the couch watching TV with their significant other by now, he assumed. He walked into Flanagan's and took a seat at the counter. There was he, and over in the corner, a family finishing off dinner and the wait staff. Other than that, the place was empty. Leanne saw him and waved. She then disappeared back into the kitchen, only to reappear with a plate. She quickly brought it over to Ryder and put it down in front of him.

"I hope you're not a vegan," she said.

Ryder admired the massive turkey and Swiss cheese sandwich. "This is for me?"

'Yes!" smiled Leanne

"Oh wow, you are too kind," Ryder gave a small smile.

"Well, eat that as we wrap it up here. I should be done in 20 minutes," Leanne explained.

'Yes, ma'am!" said Ryder, giving Leanne a sly wink.

After Leanne and her crew were done with their end-of-service procedures, she came up and checked Ryder's plate.

"Hungry were we?" she asked, looking at his picked-clean plate.

"Great sandwich, many thanks. How much do I owe ya?" Ryder asked.

"It's on the house, babe. Just for you," Leanne explained.

"Oh wow, thank you!" said Ryder 'Are there any bars open? I'll take you for a drink."

"Yes, there are bars open. Just because we live in a small town doesn't mean our bars close at 9 pm," teased Leanne.

"Fair enough," Ryder smiled again. This was what? The 3rd time in 25 years that he had smiled?

"How long until you are ready?" he asked.

"Let me get rid of this plate, and you know, give me 2 minutes," she replied.

Before Ryder knew it, Leanne was escorting him down Main Street and up some side street.

"Are you planning to abduct me and harvest my organs?" he teased.

"No, no. Don't be silly," laughed Leanne, "I'm taking you to my favorite bar."

They turned another corner, and Ryder saw some neon ahead. *So she really is taking me to a bar and not setting me up to be experimented on,* thought Ryder.

The bar turned out to be pretty cool. They had a few drinks, and Ryder checked the room to see if there was anyone who looked like they might have info on Vince. However, it was loud, and the crowd looked fairly young. Around 12, Leanne told him she had to go home. He offered to walk her back.

'So that was the Tin Cactus Dive bar," Leanne stated on their walk back to her place. "What did you think?"

"Pretty cool," said Ryder, not wanting to tell her the music was too loud and the crowd too young. Why spoil her night?

She directed Ryder through the quiet morning streets of Coyote Ridge. Her house was on the other side of Main Street, but it didn't take them long to arrive.

"Well, this is it," she announced, standing in front of a modest suburban-style home.

Ryder checked it out. It was better than anything he had ever lived in. "Pretty cool," he stated.

Before he had a chance to say any more or leave, Leanne pulled him in close and kissed him. He returned the kiss.

"Do you want to come in?" she asked.

What sort of guy doesn't want to come in when an attractive 40-something woman invites them in? Thought Ryder.

"Yeah, sure," he replied, trying not to sound too enthusiastic.

She led him past the front door and kissed him again. They barely made it to the couch before they were tearing each other's clothes off and having sex.

CHAPTER 27

Northern Arizona

KC led his troops down Highway 77. From memory, the turn off for Pine Hollow was on the right. He looked back and admired his boys. The way they all locked in and rode in close proximity to each other. One wrong move and all of them would crash. It took real skill to ride like that. He was proud of his club and proud of his dudes.

KC likened himself to an old-school general leading his men into battle. In a sense, he was. They were confronting the man who killed his brother, Kyle Ossi, back in Mexico. No club with any sense of self-respect could let one of its brothers be killed and not avenge that death. It had taken half a year, but KC had been determined for justice to be served.

It was just pure chance that one of his guys had been riding without his colors and stopped in at the motorcycle shop where the prick worked in the Northern Arizona town of Pine Hollow.

Boxer had managed to sneak a photo of the guy, and KC had gotten Frank and Brendan to confirm he was the Steel Reaper at the diner, back in Mexico. At first, KC thought they had to be mistaken, but then reality sank in; it really was him. He couldn't wait to get to Pine Hollow and destroy this fool.

KC looked up and saw the signs for a town called Ironwood Bluff coming up. He was confused. Wasn't that AFTER Pine Hollow and not before? Had he been lost in thought and missed the turn off? He gave the signal to the guys and took the exit for Ironwood. He checked his mirrors and was pleased to see the boys following after him. He downshifted as the speed limit decreased as they approached Main Street.

Looking to his right, KC spied a bar called the Iron Horse. In his mind, he thought that might have potential, so he signaled that they were coming to a stop and pulled up in front of the dive bar. He backed into the spot with his bike, heading out away from the curb. His boys followed his lead and parked up as well.

"We stopping for a drink?" asked Brendan

"What about food?" asked Mike

"We just ate in Flagstaff, you fat fuck," joked Parrot Head.

"Well, I'm hungry again," stated Mike.

"You got enough blubber to last you a month," teased Frank.

'Shut it," cursed Mike.

"Yeah, one drink," said KC.

"Why did we roll past Pine Hollow?" asked Rhino.

"Ah, cuz I figured we need to hash out a plan," lied KC.

"Yeah, good thinking, Prez," Mike replied.

The six bikers grabbed a booth, and Mike went to the bar and returned with a few pitchers of beer.

"I've got some wings coming too," Mike proudly announced.

"I'm good, thanks though," said Rhino.

As Mike started pouring everyone's drinks, KC pulled out his paper map and studied it again. Sure enough, he must have zoned out and missed the turn-off for Pine Hollow. Oh well, it was only a 20-minute ride back up the highway. No biggie. They would finish their beers and head back to Pine Hollow.

"We're probably not gonna get to town until after 6 pm now," announced Parrot Head.

"Yeah, I did that on purpose," lied KC, "Get into his head. He knows we are coming; the longer we draw it out, the more off balance this guy is going to be."

"Ah, good thinking, Prez," said Rhino 'I knew you had a reason for missing the exit."

"Always, bro," lied KC, putting his paper map back into his jacket pocket.

CHAPTER 28

Coyote Ridge, Arizona.

The rest of the week was a bit of a repeat of their first day together. Leanne would go to work, Ryder would go by Flanagan's 30 minutes before her lunch shift ended – eat food, and they would go to their make-out spot. Ryder would walk Leanne back to work, take a power nap when he got back to his motel, and meet her in the evening at the restaurant where she would feed him.

Then she would close up shop, they would hit one of the local bars for a couple of drinks and then have sex when they got home.

Ryder realized that he was getting distracted from his mission of vengeance, tracking down Vince, but kept telling himself, "Just one more day and I will move on."

That evening, after they had had sex, Leanne lay on Ryder's chest, admiring his tattoos and scars.

For whatever reason, she started to tell him about her former husband and child. Most people around town knew what had happened but never spoke about it. That was fine with Leanne, as talking about it just brought back the pain and sorrow. With Ryder, she felt she could tell him. He held her tighter in his beefy arms as she gave him the story. Instead of feeling miserable afterwards, she felt like a weight had been lifted from her soul.

Leanne then turned the subject to Ryder.

"So it's obvious you did time, what for?" she said 'If you don't mind me asking."

"I tried to rob a Weed Dispensary in California, figured it would be easier than a bank," Ryder replied 'I was wrong."

"Oh no,"

"Yeah, I got 21 years for that error," said Ryder. '21 years I'll never get back"

"What made you think to try that?" Leanne asked.

"It was my friend Vince's idea," Ryder replied. "I was hoping to get out of debt and have enough cash to start my own business."

"Oh no, when did Vince get released?" asked Leanne. "I recall you saying he came through this way some years back."

Ryder paused for a moment. He contemplated not telling her, but then figured what harm would it do to tell the truth?

"Yeah, so Vince did me dirty and got away," said Ryder.

'What? He turned state's evidence on you?" asked Leanne.

"No, worse. He knocked me out cold and left me there to be caught by the cops while he took all the money," Ryder explained.

"Your friend did that to you? OH MY GOD," said Leanne 'What kind of friend would do that?" She was mad now.

"Let me tell you. I spent 20 years asking myself the same question," Ryder replied.

"Wow, what a pair," stated Leanne, "Between the two of us, if it wasn't for bad luck, we would have no luck at all."

Ryder laughed 'Sounds like a country song!"

Leanne laughed too.

Ryder slept in the next day as Leanne went to work. She had gotten so used to him staying at her place that she was happy for him to sleep in while she got up to tackle the morning shift at Flanagan's. He tidied up around her house, then locked up and made his way back to his motel room. The walk took him about 15 minutes, and although the sun was out, it was still a fairly cool morning. It was always at least 20 degrees cooler in Coyote Ridge than down in the Valley of the Sun, where Phoenix was.

Ryder seriously considered giving up his hotel room, but thought better of it. The last thing he wanted to be accused of was latching on to a lonely widow.

When he went to Flanagans that evening, the diner was super busy. After he ate the meal Leanna had prepared for him, she suggested that he go to the bar and that she meet him there later. It was a bar Ryder had not been to before, called the Highway Haul. Leanne gave him directions and sent him on his way.

Ryder entered the Highway Haul and assessed the room. There were a few people at the tables and one old drunk at the far end of the bar. Ryder chose to sit in the middle of the bar where he could kind of keep an eye on the room through the mirrors in front of him. The bartender was an old geezer who looked like he should be milking cows on a farm as opposed to slinging drinks. In Ryder's mind, they were always the best bartenders. No nonsense guys with a never-ending supply of worldly wisdom.

He ordered a beer and a shot.

"Haven't seen you around here before," stated the grizzled old geezer 'Are you that fella that's been hanging out with our Leanne?" he asked.

"That would be me," said Ryder. "My name is Ryder. Nice to meet you."

Ryder extended his hand to shake, and the old geezer took it and shook. Good firm grip, obviously a man who had worked with his hands all his life.

'I'm Rusty," declared the old boy.

"Nice to meet you, Rusty," Ryder replied.

Rusty bought over a beer and two shots of Whiskey. He handed one to Ryder and kept one for himself.

"Whiskeys are on me, son," said Rusty 'Two bucks for the beer."

Ryder handed a $5 bill to Rusty. "Keep the change, sir."

'So you came up to our town just to see Leanne?" asked Rusty after downing his shot.

'No, I came looking for an old friend, apparently he blew through here 20 years ago," Ryder explained.

"Oh yeah? Chances are, I probably know him then," smiled Rusty, fetching two more whiskey shots.

He returned and put one shot in front of Ryder.

They both took their whiskey shots, "cheers"ed each other and downed them.

"Thank you," said Ryder, sliding the glass back over.

'Well?" said Rusty 'You got a picture of this friend of yours or what?"

"Ah, yeah. Hold on," said Ryder. He fished out his wallet and retrieved the only photo he had of Vince.

Rusty put on his reading glasses and studied the photo 'This one is you, correct?" pointing to the much younger Ryder.

"Yes, sir,"

He studied the photo some more.

"Yeahhhh," Rusty drawled, "I remember this fella. Name is Vince, right?"

Ryder nearly fell off his chair. This guy remembered him! What were the chances? He was right. His gut instinct was right. Vince had been here!

"Yes, sir," Ryder replied.

'Yeah, he came in here, must have been 20 years ago now. He wanted to buy my bar. Offered to pay cash. I told him I wasn't interested," said Rusty. "He seemed like he was in a hurry to buy."

"Oh yeah," said Ryder. Definitely sounded like Vince. 'Do you know what happened to him?"

"Yeah, I remember it like yesterday. I got a bad feeling about the guy," said Rusty

'That would be right," said Ryder, almost under his breath. 'So what happened to him?"

"I sent him on his way. Told him to try the next town over."

"Pine Hollow?" asked Ryder.

"Yes, sir," said Rusty 'That town was going through some tough times then. He would have a better chance at a quick sale in Pine Hollow," said Rusty.

'So he went to Pine Hollow for sure?" asked Ryder.

"Yeah, I believe he bought a bar in town," said Rusty.

Ryder could barely contain his excitement. Part of him felt like checking out now and riding right over to Pine Hollow. So close now. He did his best to hide his excitement from his new pal Rusty. Ryder contemplated the best way to break it to Leanne. He would think of something.

CHAPTER 29

Pine Hollow, Arizona.

Joe had mixed feelings about the cars of local teens who had come to watch the showdown between rival biker clubs. On the one hand, with so many witnesses, they were much less likely to start blasting away at him (too many witnesses). On the other hand, if a shoot-out did happen and one of the kids got clipped by a stray bullet, he knew somehow that the local sheriff would find a way to pin it all on him, regardless of them turning up in numbers, as spectators had taken some of the edge off his nerves.

What will be will be, it's all in God's hands now, Joe figured.

He checked his watch. 5.30 pm. They should be here soon. Maybe they were already in town? Trashing Clay's store? Terrorizing the locals? Should he go back and check? If he did, he ran the risk of being caught out in the open by the Dark Legion, potentially taken somewhere and tortured before being murdered. He had to stay here. Maybe they were deliberately taking their sweet time to psyche him out?

Joe paced the clearing again. As he circled back, he saw three more cars slowly approaching the car park. He tensed involuntarily. *Here we go*, he thought, taking a deep breath. *This is it. Fight or Flight.*

The three cars slowed as they entered the car park and picked out spots by the top end. Two of the vehicles drove front-first into their spots, and the third car backed into its spot. That must be them, Joe thought. Fixing to make a quick getaway after their confrontation, he imagined.

He took another breath and tried to calm his nerves. He would explain that it wasn't him who killed their guy. Of course, for young guys like this, that wouldn't be acceptable. So then he would offer to fight one of their guys. Mano vs Mano. Old school style. Even if he got a beating, it would be better than getting shot.

Joe had to question himself. Did someone somewhere feel he deserved a beating because he was left with no choice but to kill his club brother, Johnny, that evening in Mexico? Maybe? It was self-defense. He had no choice but to shoot Johnny or be killed by him. Was this his Karma to die by their hands? You take a life, and the Universe takes yours? Surely killing someone in cold blood warranted bad karma, but self-defense? Nah, cmon. That didn't seem right.

Joe realized the new arrivals were still sitting in their cars. *Come on fuckers, let's go. I'm ready for you. I'm not going to run. I'm going to stand my ground. You ready?*

He stared intently at the 3 cars. Finally, a door opened. *A woman exited the vehicle. What was this? They brought their old ladies along with them?*

Finally, the car Joe thought contained the Dark Legion Club dudes revealed its passengers, another group of college kids. *What on earth? Was this town so starved of excitement that everyone came out to watch the bike clubs go at it with each other?*

Joe was disgusted. But on the other hand, he had to remind himself that the more kids that arrived here, the harder it would be for the Dark Legion to send them home. The more witnesses, the more chance it would be a fist fight and not a massacre. Staying alive was the goal at the end of the day, and these kids pretty much guaranteed that he would survive.

Joe checked his watch again. 5.45 pm. The sun would be setting in an hour. If they arrived after sunset, it would be easier for them to pull some dirty tricks on Joe, but at the same time, he could use the darkness to his benefit, too. Regardless, he was growing impatient and wished they would get here now, so he could get on with it.

CHAPTER 30

Coyote Ridge, Arizona.

Just as Ryder was contemplating cutting out and heading back to his motel room, checking out then, heading north to the town of Pine Hollow, Leanne walked in. She hugged him in front of Rusty and asked for a light beer.

Once she was served, she grabbed Ryder by the hand and led him to a booth near the back of the bar.

"So what did you make of Rusty?" asked Leanne.

"Yeah. I love guys like that. Straight to the point, no nonsense," Ryder replied. He decided at this point not to share the news about Vince.

"He's been in this town FOREVER," Leanne replied.

"I can tell. Seems to know everything about everyone, including us," Ryder replied.

'Well, you know what they say about small towns," laughed Leanne 'Everyone knows everyone else's business."

'Yeah, you're not wrong there," said Ryder in between sips of his beer.

"One of the downsides of living in Coyote Ridge, but on the whole, I would never live anywhere else," said Leanne.

"Yeah, I get it," said Ryder.

They had one more round of drinks, then Leanne suggested they go back to her place. Ryder walked her back, and once again they had sex. This time at least, they made it to Leanne's bed first.

Afterwards, he lay on his back while she lay on his chest.

"Listen, I've got something to tell you," said Ryder softly, not wanting to cause a scene. "Rusty told me he knows where Vince is. He is in the next town over. The town of Pine Hollow,"

"Pine Hollow, my sister's husband is the Sheriff there," said Leanne. "He must know where he is."

"Probably so," Ryder replied, "But I would rather just go there and see for myself before you get law enforcement involved."

"Ah, yes. I get it," said Leanne. "Makes sense."

"Yeah, so please don't call on my behalf," said Ryder.

"So are you leaving then?" asked Leanne.

"Well, I'll go for the day and check it out, then I'll come back. I promise," said Ryder.

"You'd better!" Leanne replied. 'Otherwise I'll hunt YOU down," she joked.

"Well, how about this? I'll check out of my motel tomorrow. Ride to Pine Hollow, see if it really is Vince, then come back in a day or two. When I do, I'll come right to your place and not bother with a room. Does that work for you?" Ryder asked.

Leanne thought about it for a moment, "Ok, that's cool. Let's do that then," She soon closed her eyes and fell asleep on his tattooed and scarred chest. *Well, that settles it. Check out of the motel. Ride to Pine Hollow. Scout the town out and see if Vince still lives there.*

At least he had a plan now.

The next morning, Ryder left Leanne's house when she left for work. He made sure to grab his hidden Mossberg from under the bed, then packed his bag and rolled his scoot out into the car park. He paid his tab at the front office and checked the map before leaving Coyote Ridge. According to his calculations, it should take no more than 15 minutes to get there, heading north on the 77.

Sure enough, it wasn't long before he saw the signs for the turn off to Pine Hollow. It had to be no more than 15 minutes, according to Ryder's estimates. He figured, same process as the other towns. Roll in. Cruise the main drag. Get a feel for the place, find a motel, check in. Try to find this bar. Post up, wait until he sees the owner, and figure out if it was indeed Vince. For all he knew, Vince could have sold the bar and moved to New York City by now. A lot can change in 20 years. If that was the case, he would head right back to Leanne.

He cruised down the main street of Pine Hollow, which seemed slightly larger than Coyote Ridge, maybe by a block or two more. While keeping his eyes on the road, he tried to look out for bars. By his calculations, there had to be 3-4 in town. No problem. It wouldn't take long to figure out which one Vince owned.

Ryder had spotted a small motel at the top end of Main Street, so he pulled a U-turn when no one was coming and headed back up towards the Highway. Despite telling Leanne he would be back as soon as possible, Ryder fully realized it could be a couple of days to track down Vince and figure out the best way to get to him. He planned on returning to Coyote Ridge and Leanne, but not until justice had been served.

Ryder turned off Main Street and into the motel's car park. He shut down his bike and went into the front office, hoping to book a room for a couple of days. Unfortunately, they told him he could only have 1 night as a travel group had booked up all their rooms for the next 2 nights. Fair enough, he would have to work fast.

The room was basic but fairly affordable, so he had no complaints. He rolled his bike in through the motel door and parked it by the side of the bed. That way, he had a nice, clear walkway to the bathroom in the middle of the night if he needed to go. He had fallen over his Harley once in a drunken stupor and nearly broken his big toe. Lesson learned. Never again.

On a whim, he decided to walk up and down Main Street, maybe one or two of the bars were open already, or he might see the owner setting up for the day. He locked his motel door and the motel parking lot. Heading towards Main Street, he nearly got knocked over by two teenagers on skateboards who shot out of an alley on his right.

"Oops, sorry," said the first skater.

Ryder was about to curse them out, but thought better of it.

"No worries. Hey, you kids live in town, right?" he asked.

"Yeah, why?" asked the second skater.

"I'm looking for an old friend of mine," Ryder explained.

The two skaters looked at him for a moment. Probably contemplating whether he was a child molester or some form of weirdo.

"Here, I've got a photo of him," said Ryder, reaching for his wallet.

The first skater took a picture of Ryder. "That's me there," said Ryder, pointing to himself in the old photo.

The first skater studied it and handed it to the second skater. He looked at it and handed it back to Ryder.

'Well?" asked Ryder 'You know him."

"Sure do. That's Vince," said the first teenager.

Shit, they do know him. How? Thought Ryder.

"Yep, that's my friend Vince. How do you know him?" asked Ryder.

'Everyone knows him," the second skater replied.

'What? How?" asked Ryder, totally stunned by the kid's reply.

"Look," said both skaters at the same time, pointing behind Ryder.

He looked up to see a giant billboard across the street, "Re-elect your local Sheriff Vince Williams."

Ryder felt his knees buckle. There was Vince up on a massive Billboard. His face was fatter, his hair was thinner, but sure enough, that was him. *Sheriff? How on earth did that happen? He was the last person who should be a sheriff.*

He had to find somewhere to sit down and take this all in. Maybe back in his room? He looked for a bench to sit on down Main Street, but there wasn't one.

He walked down Main Street in a daze. He saw an open bar and went in. He sat at the counter and waited to be served. A woman came out of the back room and approached him.

"Hi there, Hun, sorry, I didn't hear you come in. Drinking already?" she asked.

"Yeah, I just need a quick beer," Ryder explained.

"Yeah, one of those mornings, eh?" she asked.

"Pretty much," Ryder replied.

They sat and chatted for a while as Ryder sipped on his beer. It was actually helping for some reason.

The bartender's name was Rosalind, and she explained to Ryder that Sheriff Vince Williams was the proud owner of a bar called the Dead Crow Saloon. Situated down the other end of Main Street. When the last Sheriff was arrested for running a crime ring, Vince gave all his regular customers free beer in exchange for promising to vote for him. That's how he swung the vote. It all made sense now. What better way to hide from law enforcement than to become law enforcement? Ryder had to tread carefully now. Vince could use any bullshit excuse against Ryder to have him locked up, possibly even sent back to prison. Ryder realized he would have to watch Vince very carefully and wait for the right moment to strike.

It also occurred to him that this must be Leanne's brother-in-law. What were the chances? She knew Vince had betrayed him, but how would she feel about Ryder killing her brother-in-law? He would worry about that when the time came.

Ryder finished his beer and decided not to get another. He needed a clear head now; more beers would just fog up his thinking. Unsure of what to do next, he figured out he should go back to his motel and plan out his next steps.

When Ryder got back to his room, the maid was just finishing up cleaning it. He waited outside in the parking lot until she was done, as he didn't want to freak her out. He nodded at her as she left, making her way to the next room down.

He sat on his bed and ran through his options. Forget his plan to avenge Vince's betrayal and go back to Leanne? How soon before she would want to introduce him to her sister and Vince? What dirty tricks would Vince do when he found out Ryder was living nearby? He would never have peace that way. Always waiting and expecting Vince to set him up again.

Kill Vince and run the risk of ruining his relationship with Leanne? She knew the pain Vince had caused him. Would she forgive him? *Probably not,* he thought.

Run away from both Vince and Leanne? Head back to California and forget the last 20 years? Ryder wasn't a runner. Running from his problems never solved anything. He always faced them head-on.

He was at a loss. A fork in the road, with no clue which way to turn.

Ryder decided to call his sister. She had been supportive of him throughout his entire incarceration and had let him stay at her and her husband's house on his release. He wasn't going to look for advice from her, but maybe just by talking things out with her, he might come up with some answers.

"Hey, Rach, it's me," said Ryder when his sister Rachel answered the phone.

'Oh, hey Ry, you okay? Where are you?" Rachel asked him.

'Yeah, I'm good. I'm in Northern Arizona," Ryder explained.

"Oh wow, your probation officer knows this?" she asked.

'All good, he told me I can just phone in until I am back," Ryder explained.

'Oh, cool. So what's in Northern Arizona? A job opportunity?" Rachel asked him.

'Well, I met a woman," said Ryder.

'Color me shocked," laughed Rachel, "You always loved the ladies."

'Yeah, yeah," Ryder replied 'But check this. I found Vince!"

"What? How?" she asked him.

"He always talked about moving to Arizona. It took some time, but I found him," said Ryder.

'Don't do anything stupid, Ry," scolded Rachel.

'I won't," Ryder lied, "But you know what he put me through."

'What about you? You have to accept some accountability for your own actions, Ry," Rachel replied.

Ryder sighed 'Okay, I do. I was on the wrong path, and if I hadn't been caught, I would have probably ended up doing more and more bad things. Who's to know for sure, though?"

"Well, that's something. At least you can acknowledge your mistakes, Ry," said Rachel.

"I do," said Ryder 'But how is it fair? He set me up and got away with this for 20 years?"

"Ry," sighed Rachel, "Life isn't fair. Sometimes you just have to sit back and let karma run its course."

Ryder had spent 20 years vowing to get revenge on Vince for his vile betrayal of his trust. He was not in the mood for any hippy dippy stuff about peace, love and karma. However, he also didn't want to get into an argument with his sister, especially since she had helped him out to the best of her abilities during his years of incarceration.

"Hey, Rach, I gotta go. I'll call you soon. Promise," Ryder replied.

"Ok, Ry. Well, stay safe and be smart," said Rachel, hanging up her phone.

Yeah, yeah, thought Ryder. Easy for her to say. She didn't lose half her life over one dumb mistake.

He checked the time on his phone. He had just enough time to call Leanne before she had to start her afternoon/evening shift at Flanagans. He debated not calling her or, at the very least, not telling her that Vince was her brother-in-law.

He decided to call her and play it by ear. He dialed her number. She answered.

"Hiii," she said, excited to hear from him.

"Hey, it's me," Ryder replied.

"Yes, I can see that. Your name comes up when you call me; it's not the 1980s anymore, babe. People don't have to answer the phone blindly, not knowing who it was on the other line," she teased.

"Yeah, yeah, very funny," said Ryder, "It's still the polite thing to do. Introduce yourself. So there, smarty pants."

Leanne laughed 'So, how's your search for that prick? Any leads?" she asked.

"Yeah, about that," said Ryder.

'Wait! You found him? Wow, that was quick," she exclaimed.

"Yeah, it wasn't hard, trust me," said Ryder. "His face was on a giant billboard in town."

"Wait, what?" asked Leanne.

"Are you ready for this?" he asked.

"Uh, I'm not sure what you mean?" said Leanne, slightly confused.

"The man I am looking for is your brother-in-law," said Ryder.

"What? Sheriff Williams is Vince? Oh, Shit, we always called him Vin. I'm so sorry, Ryder. I never put two and two together. Oh god!" Leanne replied.

"Yeah, you can imagine how I felt," Ryder replied. "I don't know what to do."

"You can't kill him, babe!" Leanne replied, "Oh god. Just come home now. Please"

"I can't do that, baby," Ryder replied. 'I just can't"

There was a long, uncomfortable silence on the phone.

"You still there?" asked Leanne finally.

"Yeah, I'm here," said Ryder.

"What are you going to do, Ryder?" Leanne asked softly.

"I don't know. I honestly don't know. I need a night to think on it," said Ryder.

"Please don't do anything stupid," said Leanne. It sounded like she was going to cry.

"I won't," said Ryder, not sure if that was the truth or a lie. "Just give me 24 hours to think about everything."

"Okay," said Leanne. It felt like she wanted to say more.

"Look, do one thing for me," said Ryder

"What's that?" asked Leanne

'Just don't call your sister or her husband, okay?" said Ryder. 'I don't need him sending me back to prison on some b.s. Charges. Okay?"

"Ok," said Leanne

'Just give me 24 hours and I'll get back to you," said Ryder.

"You promise?" asked Leanne.

"Yeah. I promise," said Ryder, hanging up the phone.

Great, now he had two women mad at him. He was more confused now than before he made the call to her. He understood she knew him as the kind-hearted local Sheriff Williams. But she didn't lose 20 years of her life due to his treachery. It was different for him than for her.

Ryder had some thinking to do. The only answer was to go to a bar and have a few drinks. What was the name of the bar he owned? The Dead Something Saloon? Perhaps he could go in there and drink; maybe he would even get a chance to see Vince up close. Would he recognize Ryder? He doubted it. It had been over 20 years, and he looked drastically different. Besides, Ryder was looking for him. He highly doubted Vince would even be thinking of Ryder. He would risk it.

He grabbed his jacket but left his backpack with the Mossberg in his room. He decided he wouldn't make any swift decisions and just go and check the place out.

Wandering back down Main Street, he found the bar on the last block. The Dead Crow Saloon. That was the one. He took a breath and entered the dive bar. There were a few people at the booths and a couple of old drunks propping up the end of the bar. Rock music played on the juke box, and a white kid who looked like a modern-day hippy was slinging drinks at the bar.

Ryder took a seat at the bar. He usually preferred the back booth, where he could see who was coming and going, but a couple sat there. He would have to use the mirrors behind the racks of liquor to keep his eyes open. He ordered a beer and a shot and started to drink. The hippy kid turned out to be kinda cool. After a couple of beers, the couple at the back booth left. Ryder got up, took his beer and shot to the booth and kept an eye out for Vince as he drank.

CHAPTER 31

Ironwood Bluff, Arizona.

KC made the Dark Legion boys finish up their drinks and got everyone back on the road within 10 minutes. He had no clue how the night was going to play out, but he figured they at least needed to check into their motel rooms now. Knowing these small po dunk towns, undoubtedly, if you showed up late, they would give your room to someone else. He was not planning on sleeping out in the open tonight, screw that.

"Cmon, boys, it's time to ride," said KC as they were mounting up their bikes. 'We gotta check into the motel and go kick some Steel Reaper ass. Who's with me?"

All of them cheered.

As KC waited for his bike to warm up, he reflected on the club's response to getting revenge on this Steel Reaper. First off, why did he have to take it upon himself to lead this pack? The Utah boys should have administered shift justice down in Mexico. Secondly, if he hadn't put pressure on everyone to use every one of their connections to find out where this Reaper scumbag had disappeared to, would they have found the guy? No, of course not. It was always left up to him. *Well,* thought KC, *I guess that's why I am the club president and they are not.* Still, it irked him that none of them had the initiative to step up. Take charge for once, make some decisions of their own. It wouldn't hurt. Plus, it would take some of the pressure off him.

He had worked hard for the club, he had done his time, earned his stripes, and if anything, things were now tougher for him than when he was coming up. Everyone was an idiot. Did I.Q. drop since he became a prospect? *The exhilarating thrill of wielding power can be greatly diminished when you're surrounded by fools,* KC thought to himself. *Where was the glory in being a leader when you spent 90% of your time keeping a bunch of goofs in check? Things would change when he got home. That was for sure.*

This time, he didn't miss the turn off for Pine Hollow. There was the sign, 2 miles ahead. He must have been deep in thought earlier to completely miss the turn off. Oh well. That was on him. No biggie.

According to his map, the motel should be up ahead on the right. He saw the Neon sign telling him where the motel was. Totally retro sign – looked like it hadn't been updated since the 1950s.

KC and the boys parked up near the front office and filed in to check into their pre-booked rooms. To his relief, the clerk had not given their rooms away to anyone else. He told his crew they had 5 minutes to dump their gear, take a piss, freshen up, whatever and then they had to hit the road.

According to his sources, the bike shop was on the same side of Main Street but at the other end of town. Judging by the size of Pine Hollow, it shouldn't take them more than a few minutes to get down there and handle business.

To his surprise and his pleasure, most of the guys were in and out of their rooms in two minutes. Only that fatty Mike was still in his room.

"Someone go grab Mike," KC ordered.

Rhino shrugged and walked down the car park towards Mike's room. He knocked on the door. No reply. He pounded on the door, stopped and listened and then returned to where the rest of the club was waiting.

"Well?" asked KC.

Rhino shook his head 'He's taking a dump."

"Typical," groaned Parrot Head.

A couple more minutes passed, and finally Mikey appeared.

"All done?" teased Brendan.

'Hey, when nature calls, nature calls," Mike replied 'Besides, it's far better to take a dump in your own private restroom than some dive bar, right?"

'Whatever. Let's just get going," snapped KC 'We're burning daylight here."

"How far to his motorcycle shop?" asked Frank

'It's down the other end of Main Street," KC explained. 'I reckon it will be no more than 2-3 minutes.

From what my sources told me, it's not his shop, though. He just works there."

"He won't be working there much longer, if ya get me," chuckled Parrot Head.

"Okay, enough talk, let's roll, boys," said KC, starting up his scooter.

As they rolled through town, KC couldn't help but notice how few people were on the streets. It was only early evening, and he saw someone who looked like an old geezer walking up Main Street. It didn't seem like a ghost town. So where was everyone?

KC scanned ahead. The next block was the final block of Main Street. He blipped and downshifted, slowing his pace. This was in the moment he had prepped for since learning where this Reaper had been hiding out. He had rehearsed what he was going to say to the guy a hundred times, what he was going to do. This was his moment. His day to cement his legacy in Dark Legion History.

He waved at the boys to pull over. He kinda figured out where the store was. They pulled up in front of the hardware store next door and looked around. Again, so few people around, so few stores open. *Was it a public holiday he had forgotten about?*

"Where is everyone?" asked Rhino.

"Yeah. Dunno. I was thinking the same thing while riding in," KC replied. "To be fair, though, I did tell my guy to spread it around town that we were coming. Just to instill fear. Ya know?"

"Yeah, good thinking. It's like everyone closed up early and went home," Rhino replied.

KC swaggered towards the motorcycle shop. With so few people around, he could shoot the Reaper in his shop, and there would probably be no witnesses. He grabbed the door handle and pushed. Locked. WTF!

It was only then that he noticed the sign.

"Hey, check this," he told his boys, "He's waiting for us in a field just outside of the city limits."

'What a coward," scoffed Mike. "Couldn't stand and face us like a man"

"Weak," sneered Parrot Head.

"Well. Let's fire up the bikes and go find this scum bag," said KC, "By the sound of things, it's probably only a 5-minute ride away."

"Let's go, boys," said Rhino.

"Where are we supposed to meet him?" asked Brendan

"It's some rest stop, open field, apparently," KC explained.

"Could be a trap?" asked Mike.

'I doubt it, from what I heard, even his own club wants nothing to do with him," KC explained.

"Ahh, got ya," said Mike.

"Anyways, enough yapping. Let's go already," shouted KC.

KC waited until the boys were all ready and then pulled out of Main Street. According to the simple diagram left on the note taped to the shop front door, it should be 2 miles down the road and on the left. Easy to spot, apparently. Would there be a sign? What should he look out for? He wasn't sure, but he couldn't afford to blow it like he did when they made their initial approach to Pine Hollow.

No sooner had KC got into top gear than he noticed a clearing up ahead on the left. Was this it? As he slowed down to check it out, he realized there were about 10 cars there. Was Mikey right? Was this a trap? As he got closer, he realized it was mainly high school kids. Looked like they were partying. What was this Steel Reaper chump playing at?

He blipped his throttle as he downshifted. This couldn't be the spot, could it?

He found a spot on the other side of the dirt car park and pulled up. All the teenagers partying cheered as he shut off his bike. Maybe this was it? They had been waiting for him and the boys to arrive. Was life really that boring in a small town? Regardless, they seemed excited to see him and the Dark Legion.

The rest of the club pulled up next to him. Judging by their faces as they pulled off their helmets, they were as confused as he was.

"What the fuck, bro?" asked Rhino.

'You tell me," said KC.

Mike slung his helmet down on his right handlebar and stormed over to the carloads of teens.

'Hey, hey! You can't be here. There's gonna be a fight," he shouted at them.

'We know! That's why we are here," one of the male teens shouted back at Mike.

"Ya gotta get out of here," Mike replied.

'We ain't going anywhere," said another older male 'This is our town. We're staying."

Mikey looked back at KC, exasperated.

KC shrugged. The look on his face was "Let 'em stay."

The rest of his crew slung off their helmets. KC saw Rhino check for the pistol in his riding vest.

"Where is this piece of shit?" Asked Parrot Head.

KC grabbed him and turned him to look away from the car park.

'I reckon that's him," he said as an older biker approached them with his hands in the air.

"Stay back," shouted Rhino to the older dude.

"I'm unarmed," the biker announced.

"We're not," shouted Mikey.

"My name's Joe," the older biker shouted.

'Yeah. I know all about you scumbag," shouted KC 'You killed one of my boys in Mexico and now you're gonna die."

"I didn't kill anyone," Joe replied, "My bro Johnny did, and he has since died."

'Bullshit!" shouted KC. He wasn't so sure, though. He turned to Mike, Brendan and Frank.

'That's the guy, right?' he hissed at the trio.

'That's him," Mike and Brendan answered in unison. 'I can still see him in the car park holding a pistol on us," Mike added.

"I didn't shoot your guy," Joe shouted, "That was Johnny, remember?"

"Hey, I think he might be right," Frank said to KC. "It was his bro"

KC looked at Mike and Brendan. "Is he right?" he hissed.

"I dunno," said Mikey.

'Fuck, now that you mention it, Frank might be right," Brendan replied.

KC swore under his breath. These fucking idiots. Still, this dude was with the guy who killed Kyle. Guilt by association. Someone had to pay, and it might as well be this Joe character.

"See, I told ya," shouted Joe.

"Nah, nah, there's no proof your boy is dead. Besides, you are here now. Someone has to pay," shouted KC, "Guess what? It's gonna be you."

"I'm telling you he is dead," Joe shouted back at them.

"Says you! We have no proof of that, except for your word," said KC, "You're a Steel Reaper, you're the only Reaper here. Therefore, you have to pay"

Joe stepped closer to the Dark Legion guys.

"Look, I didn't kill your brother. I'm sorry for your loss," said Joe. "I didn't run because I'm not guilty, okay?"

"Bullshit, you didn't run because you're too old to run," snapped KC.

Joe was about to say something back at the apparent leader of the Dark Legion, but a vehicle pulling into the car park distracted him.

KC and the boys turned to see what the old biker was looking at. A Sheriff's vehicle was pulling into the property.

"Oh, so you set this up to protect your ass?" said KC accusingly to Joe.

"Of course not. I don't have anything to do with law enforcement," Joe shouted at KC.

The Sheriff was getting out of his SUV and walking towards the bikers.

'Evening fellas," Sheriff Williams greeted the Dark Legion boys.

"We're just having a friendly discussion here," KC replied.

"Yeah, right, and I'm Ronald Reagan," Sheriff Williams replied. "Look, whatever beef you fellas have with this old geezer. I don't care. I'm staying out of it."

"Okay," KC replied.

"I'm just here to tell you, no guns and no getting these good townsfolk injured," said Sheriff Williams. "One of these people gets hurt, and you're all going to jail."

KC stared at the Sheriff blankly. *Was this fool for real? He's happy to let them fight as long as those kids don't get shot? Well, okay then.*

Sheriff Williams turned and walked back to the crowd. One of the high school kids handed him a beer, and he cracked it open.

Damn, this guy doesn't give a fuck thought KC. *Drinking beers with underage kids. That wouldn't fly back to California; that was for sure.*

"You heard the Sheriff. Pick one of your guys and let him and me sort it out between us," said Joe. "No weapons"

"Give us a minute," said Brendan, walking towards the rest of the Dark Legion, who were in a huddle.

"Frank should fight him," blurted out Mikey.

"Why do I have to fight him?" asked Frank. "Just cuz I have muscle and am not covered by a layer of fat like you?"

"Fuck you, I'm not fat," hissed Mikey.

"Shut up, you two," commanded KC. "One of you three should fight him, since Kyle died on your watch."

"The dude had a gun," whined Mike 'What did you want? For the 3 of us to get shot, too?"

"Well, you should have had guns, too. Duh," said KC in disgust.

"Well, Frank should fight him then," said Brendan, "He's the best fighter of the 3 of us."

"Bro, what the fuck!?!!," snapped Frank.

"That settles it. Frank, go kick his ass," commanded KC.

"Fuck you guys," said Frank.

The Dark Legion boys broke out of their huddle.

"Frank here is going to fight you," KC explained to Joe, stepping closer to the Steel Reapers biker.

'Fine, whatever," Joe replied, "Like I said, I didn't kill your brother, but I'm not going to run from you. For better or for worse"

"Yeah, you said that," KC replied.

"Then no matter the outcome. We are even. Right?" asked Joe.

"Yeah, I guess," said KC 'That's fair."

Frank took off his riding vest and shirt. The townsfolk who had shown up for the fight inched closer. Sheriff Vince Williams hung towards the back of the crowd. The spectators were excited. Finally, they were going to see an ass whooping.

Joe assessed his opponent as he approached the clearing. While at least 20 years younger than Joe, he was also muscular and well-built. Were those "show" muscles or legitimate muscles? Was he just a bodybuilder, or did he practice Brazilian jiu-jitsu daily? Did he have any fight experience, though? Joe thought for a moment. Most great street fighters had decent size but not that much definition. There was a good chance this guy was more of a bodybuilder after all. If it came down to a bench pressing contest, this dude would win all day, every day, thought Joe. Fighting? Maybe he had a chance. Joe figured his best shot was to go for a fast knockout and not get into a wrestling match with the younger man.

The younger biker (apparently named Frank) now stood across from Joe with his fists raised, covering his face. If he goes for a jab, it means he has had some boxing training, thought Joe. If he goes for the wild right chances, then he has no training.

The crowd cheered – sensing blood in the water.

The Dark Legion boys screamed at their fight, "Let's fucking gooo," and 'Fuck him up." Joe was undeterred and focused on Frank's body language. Trying to get a clue what he would try.

The two fighters circled each other. Who would swing first? Just to test his opponent, Joe feinted a left jab. As suspected, Frank's reaction time was slow. Inexperienced. Joe had a chance after all.

Frank took the bait – he swung with a wild right that Joe easily stepped out of the way of. He countered with a quick uppercut that connected immediately with Frank's jaw. He must have hit Frank right on the button because Frank collapsed like a sack of potatoes into the dirt. He was out for the count.

The crowd of spectators oohed and ahhed. Were they expecting a 10-round boxing match with a referee? Were they expecting a scripted main event fight like pro wrestling? This was real life. Most fights Joe had been in were over in seconds. That was real life.

'What the fuck," shouted KC in disgust.

Mike and Brendan ran to check on their club brother, who was still out cold.

"Bullshit!" shouted KC 'You cheated!"

"What? How did I cheat? You choose your man, and I fought him. We had a deal," Joe countered.

"Nah, nah, you did something," said KC, "Brass knuckles or something."

Joe held out both hands to show there was nothing concealed in either. "Where's my weapon? See nothing there!" he exclaimed.

"I dunno how, but you did.," shouted KC in a rage 'We demand a rematch."

"You're kidding. I fought your guy. It's done," said Joe, "Cmon now."

KC seemed confused. Like he didn't know how to act or what to say next, it was obvious he hadn't expected his man to go down so easily. That said, somehow Joe didn't feel like this was over just yet.

'Who wants a rematch?" asked KC, turning to the crowd like he was some form of Roman Emperor and Joe was a gladiator champion.

"YESSS," the entire crowd roared.

Fuck thought Joe, *that crowd isn't satisfied.*

"I SAID.. WHO WANTS A RE-MATCH?" shouted KC like he was a rock singer working his audience.

Again, every single one of them cheered.

"You see, old man. Your fans want to see you fight again," sneered KC to Joe.

"This was not what we agreed. But fine, you agree this is the last match, and I'll play along," said Joe. He resigned himself to at least one more fight.

"Ok, agreed," KC replied. "Gimme a second, would ya?" he turned his back on Joe and got into yet another huddle with the remaining Dark Legion bikers.

"I've been thinking," said Mikey, "You should fight him."

'What? Me? Why?" asked KC, incredulous at what he was hearing.

"Well, you are the club president," Brendan. "Effective leadership comes from the top, you know."

"He's got you there," added Parrot Head.

"Nonsense, the best fighter should fight him," KC countered. "In medieval times, the King had a knight who would protect his honor. One of you guys should step up."

"Well, maybe that's true," said Rhino, "But that was medieval times. This is the modern age."

KC was furious. This was tantamount to mutinous talk. Trouble was, he honestly didn't know who was the best fighter out of them.

"Cmon, KC, you got this. Look at that fucker. He's older than dirt," said Parrot Head encouragingly, "Rip his fucking head off."

KC looked over his shoulder. Maybe he could take the old guy? Truth be told, most of the fights he had been in as an adult, he had always made sure his opponent was smaller and weaker than him. Or he was safe in the knowledge that his club brothers had his back. Sure, this guy was old, but it looked to him as if the guy could put up a decent fight.

'Cmon, KC, you got this," added Rhino. "Two hits are all that's needed. You hit him and he hits the dirt."

Mikey laughed at Rhino's little joke. "Cmon, Prez, kick his ass."

"What's the hold up, fellas?" asked Joe

'Hold on a sec," Mikey replied to the Steel Reaper.

Joe stood in the middle of the field, keen to get this over with. He stared aggressively over at the huddle of Dark Legion bikers, wishing his eyes would bore holes into them. The fact that they had not yet chosen a fighter was a good sign to him. If they had doubts, then he had a chance to win this.

The crowd of spectators was getting restless.

'Cmon, hurry up and fight," one male shouted at the Dark Legion bikers.

'What's the hold up?" shouted another male onlooker.

Joe was kind of enjoying the harassment of the Dark Legion. The more they were hurried along, the more likely they would make a mistake.

"Cmon, man, just do it," urged Mikey. "We don't want to look soft in front of these local yokels."

"Fuck them," hissed KC, "I'll decide who fights the old fart and when!"

Frank was finally coming to. "What the hell happened?" he asked, wiggling his jaw and then rubbing his head. "Where are we?"

Mikey rushed over to where Frank was lying on the grass 'You alright, bro?"

"I dunno to be honest. My jaw hurts, and I don't feel good. What happened?"

"You fought the old guy, and he got a lucky punch on you?" Mikey explained.

"I fought my dad? Why would I do that?" asked Frank, clearly still out of it.

"No, the Steel Reaper who killed Kyle," Mikey explained.

"Wait, Kyle's dead?" asked Frank.

'Damn dude, he died 6 months ago. Are you sure you are okay?" asked Mikey.

"I dunno man, I feel like I am going to throw up. Got any water?" he asked.

"Lie back down. I'll go and find you some," Mikey instructed his fallen friend.

Mike ran up to the townsfolk who were having an impromptu party in the car park.

'Hey. Hey. Anyone got any water?" he asked.

Some of the attendees looked around, confused. *Who would bring water to a tailgate party?*

"I've got a beer you can have," one guy offered.

Realizing he probably wasn't going to get a better offer than that. Mikey accepted and returned to Frank with the cold beer.

"Cmon, KC, you got this, bro. Not just for the club but for Kyle and Frank," said Rhino.

"Yeah, look at Frank, he's not right," said Parrot Head. "You can't let him get away with rocking poor Frankie like that."

KC looked over at Mikey, who was tending to the dazed Frank. *What if the old fart clocked him that hard, too?* He had just finished paying off his last dental bill; the last thing he needed was to get his teeth knocked out.

"Fine. I'll fight 'em. Just make sure he doesn't try any funny stuff," snapped KC.

'You got it, bro," Rhino replied. Patting his gun in his vest pocket.

KC took off his leather jacket and his t-shirt. When he did this, one of the female spectators whistled and cheered. KC smiled there for a moment, trying to calm his nerves.

He walked away from his club brothers and approached Joe.

"Okay, let's do this, old man," said KC, holding up his fists to protect his face but keeping his elbows nice and tucked in to protect from rib shots.

Joe squared off against the newcomer. The fact that they took so long to pick a fighter gave him some confidence that he could win the fight. With all that said, he was still wary about getting too confident. In a street fight, anyone could beat anyone else at any given time. All it takes is one lucky shot.

The spectators, seeing a new fight, had started all began cheering and hollering.

"WOOOO," one shouted.

"Let's fucking goooooo," shouted another. Overjoyed to finally see another biker fight.

Joe and KC squared up and started circling each other. Joe launched a couple of jabs more to gauge the distance between him and the younger biker than to do any damage. He wanted to feint him out and see what skills the new challenger had up his sleeve. One thing was for certain: the new guy was taking his time. There would be no wild rights from this guy.

They circled each other again. The crowd was hooting and hollering, eager for bloodshed. KC let loose a right cross that Joe blocked. He replied with a tight rib shot into KC's left side. Joe knew he had hurt the guy.

KC winced but was adamant about not showing pain. He would definitely be feeling it come the morning, that was for sure. He advanced on the aging biker, wanting to keep him on the back foot. Joe circled again, staying out of reach of KC's right fist.

This time, KC let fly a left jab, trying to calculate the distance between Joe and himself. Joe easily blocked it, but didn't see an opening to strike out against KC again. He would wait. He had time. He figured that, as an older guy who knew how to fight, he would hit harder but was far more likely to gas out earlier than his younger attacker. It was important that he didn't exhaust himself unnecessarily. He kept his breathing regulated in through the nose and out through the mouth. So far, he felt his odds of winning were pretty good. That was one advantage of being older: more real-world experience.

The pair traded a few more blows, with neither party getting the upper hand over the other. Just for a microsecond, Joe took his eyes off KC to see if the Sheriff was still watching (he was), and at that moment, a right hook from the younger fighter caught him on his left temple. It rocked Joe, but could have been much worse. All it actually served to do was make him angry. Joe retaliated with a quick left jab that caught KC right over his eye and a vicious right that connected with KC's mouth. Joe heard an audible "crack" as he made contact, either breaking teeth or bone. When he pulled his hand back, it was bloodied.

The crowd cheered at this.

KC put his hand to his mouth, pulling it away and seeing blood. Joe knew he had hurt the younger fighter. KC's right eye was starting to swell up, too. The tide was turning. It seemed Joe now had the advantage. He looked to press it harder. He circled KC looking for another opening.

To his credit, while clearly rocked by the older biker's punches, KC was not going down without a fight. He kept his eye on Joe and moved in closer, threw a few combinations and scooted out of the way before Joe could counter. Fair enough, the kid had some footwork. Joe came forward, faked a right cross, which made KC pull his head away, and Joe then followed up with a left jab that connected with KC's nose. The jab is a very underrated move in boxing and could do some serious damage when thrown properly.

He heard the cartilage in KC's nose crack as he made contact. KC staggered back, slightly losing his balance.

The crowd oohed and ahhed when they saw the blood gushing from KC's severely damaged nose. Joe now knew he had this. With his broken nose, KC's breathing would now have to come through his mouth, making him gasp out much more easily.

KC was badly hurt now, but still not throwing in the towel. His world was rocked, but Joe had to admit the kid had heart. In another life, maybe another time, these two could have been friends, but not today. He circled KC, looking for another opening to finish the younger opponent off.

KC came forward towards Joe, throwing a wild round of punches which Joe easily blocked. KC was gassing out now, having a hard time breathing with his broken nose and struggling to see through his right eye, which was slowly swelling shut. He stepped back, contemplated his next move and attempted a flying knee towards Joe's abdomen. Joe tried to side-step the incoming onslaught, but KC's right knee still clipped his guts. Not as bad as it could have been. KC grabbed hold of Joe's right shoulder with his left arm and unleashed a flurry of blows with his right arm to Joe's body. To counter, Joe got in close and let loose an upper cut to KC's chin. KC stepped back, struggling to stay on his feet. Joe moved in to finish off the younger biker when he felt a hard blow across his back. As he stumbled forward, he turned to see one of the Dark Legion guys wielding a large tree branch. He had clearly realized his precious leader was about to be finished off and had come to his rescue.

Joe turned to tackle the overweight assailant and felt another crack across his right shoulder; another of the Dark Legion guys had joined in the attack with a large tree branch as well. Joe was already tired, and fighting two younger men with branches was not on his bingo card for today. He staggered to get out of the way as the fat guy swung again, connecting with Joe's left forearm. He was going to lose the fight if this kept up any longer.

CHAPTER 32

Pine Hollow, Arizona.

Ryder heard someone close to his bed. What the fuck? He reached for his hidden shank. It wasn't there. How did this person get into his cell? He hadn't had a cell in at least 6 months. Was it one of the prison guards? He struggled to shake the sleep out of his brain.

"Sir, Sir. Sorry to wake you, but it's way past your checkout time," said the female voice.

Huh? Thought Ryder. *I'm not locked up?*

It took him a moment to realize that he was in his motel room and not back in the penitentiary.

'Wait, what?" he asked.

"Sir, I've been knocking for a few minutes now. You were meant to check out at 11 am," the maid explained.

It was all coming back to him now. He closed out the bar last night and staggered home. He was never a big drinker, and years of sobriety in lock up, plus being older than he was 20 years ago, put him out of practice with heavy drinking. He must have slept through his wake-up call.

"Sorry, sorry," said Ryder 'Sorry, ma'am, I had a late night. If you can give me 5 minutes, I'll get out of the room."

"Okay, thank you. I have to clean the room before the next patrons check in," she explained, backing out of the room.

Fuck, amateur mistake. Ryder was glad he hadn't attacked her, thinking she was a prison assailant. Try explaining that to a judge.

He took a quick piss, brushed his teeth and started to gather his things. He made sure his Mossberg was loaded and tucked it into his backpack with his clothes and toiletries. He pulled on his clothes, checked his bike and wheeled it out the front door. He could see the maid's cart out front of the room next door to his.

'All finished," he shouted 'Sorry for the delay."

He propped his bike up and headed to the front office to hand in his room key and settle up.

After apologizing to the desk clerk for the late check-out, he bought a cold soda from the vending machine to hydrate. His mouth was dry, and his head hurt slightly. Considering the amount of booze he had put away, he was surprised he wasn't hugging the toilet bowl.

After pounding the soda, Ryder felt a little bit better. He decided to risk grabbing a quick breakfast. The more grease, the better. It would help mop up all the booze in his system before staking out the Sheriff's station.

He hit the nearest diner and ordered bacon and eggs with some home fries and toast. As he was waiting for the cook to prep his meal, he polished off two large glasses of iced water and half a pot of coffee. Yep, definitely dehydrated. As soon as his waitress served his meal, he asked for the check so that he could cut out the moment he was done. Why wait to try and grab her attention later when he needed to leave? He was already running late. He inhaled his breakfast in record time and downed the last of his coffee. He was now good to go. Well, as good as he would be for the rest of the day. I

He left the diner and jumped on his Harley. From memory, the Sheriff's station was 3 blocks away on a side street running parallel to Main Street. He cruised the streets in the direction he thought the station was and quickly found it. Ryder rode further up to a disused warehouse a block and a half up and pulled into the loading dock. The warehouse looked like it hadn't been used in at least a year, with weeds breaking through cracks in the concrete. He pulled behind a low wall and positioned himself in view of the Sheriff's station car park. If someone were to come out and stare back up the street at him, it would look like he was simply a short guy standing behind the wall, his bike completely hidden from that angle.

Although he looked nothing like he did back in the early 2000s, having Vince see a guy on a Harley staking out the station might help his foe put two and two together. He sat, he watched, and he waited. There was an old Toyota Camry and one Sheriff's vehicle in the car park. How many people worked there? Was Vince in there? What if he was out on assignment? He could sit here for the rest of the day and be none the wiser. It was a chance he would have to take. He assumed perhaps one deputy, one receptionist/dispatch person and Vince.

He checked his phone. It was now after 3 pm. Had he blown it by drinking so much last night? He watched and he waited. 30 minutes later, another Sheriff's vehicle pulled into the car park. Ryder found himself involuntarily tensing. Was this Vince? What if he couldn't make out who was getting out at this distance?

All his worries and concerns were proven unfounded. He could clearly see that it wasn't Vince. A short, overweight, uniformed cop walked around the vehicle and into the back entrance of the station. So did that mean Vince was already inside? Maybe he should call the station and find out? He recalled that these days, if someone calls law enforcement and hangs up, they can trace the call. In the instance of an old person and a home invasion, say, they can trace the call and come to that person's rescue. He couldn't risk it. He would sit and he would wait.

Ryder's earliest thirst came back to haunt him. All that soda, coffee and iced water were now wanting to get out. He looked for an appropriate place to piss. He hopped off his bike and went down the side of the disused warehouse. If someone (a nosey neighbor or a cop) were to pull up right on the street now, he would be seen, but he had no choice. He had to risk it. After taking a leak, he quickly hurried back to his bike and his scouting position. Worried that in the moment he was away, Vince would take off for the day, he was relieved to see both squad cars still in the yard. Hopefully, he had emptied his bladder enough that he wouldn't run the risk of missing Vince later in the afternoon.

Ryder's patience was rewarded when, just after 6 pm, Vince appeared. Despite putting on an extra 15-20 lbs since Ryder had last seen him, Vince still had the same funny walk that he had as a teenager. That was definitely him. How the fuck did this guy become a cop? Ryder shook his head in disgust. Local law enforcement must be desperate if this was the best they had.

Vince was talking to someone who stood in the rear doorway to the Sheriff's station. Ryder was too far away to see who it was or what they were saying. Was he saying goodbye for the night? Was he assigning the deputy some trivial tasks to keep him busy while Vince was away? Who knew? It didn't matter. He was going to follow his former friend and, once and for all, get revenge on him

183

for his traitorous behavior all those years ago. Justice would be served. He started his bike and waited for Vince to leave the car park. It was show time.

Ryder made sure to stay as far back as he dared, trailing Vince in his cop car. He doubted Vince was expecting him after all these years, but he didn't want to take any chances. As far as Ryder could tell, Vince was just riding his beat. Let the police presence in town be felt. It certainly didn't feel like Vince was in any hurry to get wherever he was going. Finally, after cruising the majority of the suburban part of town, Vince turned his cop car towards Main Street. He started on the top end near the motel that Ryder had been staying at and slowly drove down the block.

He pulled up at a hardware store a block down from the diner that Ryder had eaten in earlier this afternoon and parked. From his vantage point a block away, Ryder could clearly see the Sheriff's vehicle, and he made up his mind not to get any closer, for now. He had no need to start a confrontation with the traitorous Vince when there were numerous eyewitnesses about.

Speaking of eye witnesses, as Ryder was waiting, it did strike him. *Where is everyone?* It seemed like half the town had disappeared. Normally, at this hour, there were a lot more people up and down Main Street. *Must be a sporting event or something,* he figured.

Just as Ryder was starting to get impatient, Vince came out of the hardware store with a big smile on his face. I'm glad someone is enjoying themselves, thought Ryder grimly. He's probably been laughing and joking for the last 20 years, while I have been languishing in hell, that treacherous fuck. Vince got back in his squad car and started it up. It was time to move again.

Vince's cop car indicated, and he slowly pulled out from his parking spot in front of the hardware store. He slowly cruised down Main Street like he didn't have a care in the world. *If only he knew,* thought Ryder.

At the last block of Main Street, Vince's vehicle slowed down and pulled into a spot. On the angle he was on, Ryder couldn't see which storefront it was. It looked like the store was closed, and Vince was studying something in the window. Ryder wondered what it was. Moments later, Vince shook his head, turned, jumped back in his SUV and took off. Ryder was torn. Part of him wanted to follow Vince right away, and the other part of him was curious to check out the storefront and see what Vince was looking at. It must have been fairly important, judging by the man's reaction.

Ryder kicked his bike into gear and slowly released the clutch as he rolled down towards the storefront. Just as he got close, he saw Vince's vehicle disappear around a curve in the road ahead. He would have to risk losing him to see what the store was. It was a motorcycle shop! Before even shutting off his bike, he could see a sign taped to the front door. He jumped off his motorcycle and went to read it.

Ryder read the sign and raced back to his bike. So he now knew where Vince was heading, apparently only a couple of miles up the road. This was good. No, this was great. Vince would be miles out of town, with no witnesses, which would be perfect. This was the place to waste him. Years and years of vowing revenge were finally coming to fruition. Today. Now. It was really happening. Ryder could barely contain his excitement. He powered up his hog and took off after Vince.

After leaving the last block of Main Street, things got very rural fast. Large pine trees are to his right, and open farmland is to his left. How would he know where the meeting spot was? Ryder assumed he would have to hope and spot the Sheriff's vehicle parked to know exactly where Vince was headed. He rode another mile before spotting a large clearing ahead on his left. Looked like some type of rest area. This had to be it. As he got closer, he was horrified to see the sheer volume of cars parked there. What was going on? He blipped down the gears, and as he slowed, he spotted Vince's Sheriff's vehicle parked next to a bunch of Ford trucks. So that's where the townsfolk had gotten to! Everyone was here for a fight or confrontation of some form.

This had thrown a wrench into the works. Ryder wasn't expecting an audience. He slowly rolled into the lot and found a place near the gate in case he needed to make a quick break for it. No one had noticed him yet. Whatever was going on down in the field below had everyone transfixed. Ryder shut down his bike but kept his key in the ignition for a hasty getaway. He pulled his Mossberg from his backpack and jammed it into his riding vest. Anyone examining Ryder would instantly notice he had something shoved down his jacket, but he didn't care, at least not yet. He gave the weapon a complete once-over, satisfied it was ready for action. Now, where was Vince?

CHAPTER 33

Pine Hollow, Arizona.

Joe was losing the fight. It doesn't matter how young, how well-trained you are, or your level of fitness; fighting 3 different assailants at once was next to impossible outside of an '80s kung fu movie. Heck, even in those Bruce Lee films of the 1970s, the opponents would line up and attack old." Bruce one at a time instead of bum-rushing him. He had to think of something and fast.

He twisted and spun out of the way of the next branch swing from the fat Dark Legion attacker. He grabbed Fatty's arm, pushed it back against the man, and shoved him into his buddy, who was also wielding a tree branch. The pair went down in a tangle of denim and leather. Joe spun in time to see KC about to unleash a wild right at him. He blocked KC's right and countered with a hard right to KC's jaw, which made a sickening crunch when it connected. KC's legs buckled under him as he collapsed in the dirt like a sack of manure. The crowd cheered. Joe figured that he must have hit that little button. The nerve that runs between the skull and the jawbone. Even just a light tap in the right place on the jaw was like the button that you used for a computer restart. No matter what work you had going on with your computer, it was erased as the device shut down and eventually reopened. That had happened to KC.

At least now the odds were a little more fair. Only 2 on 1 now and not 3 on 1. Joe was relieved that most of the younger generation didn't have much training or experience in the way of fighting. That said, if any of the Dark Legion club guys were trained in mixed martial arts, he would probably be the one lying there now with all his arms and legs broken. Trying to fight a guy well-versed in Brazilian Jiu-Jitsu was like trying to fight a boa constrictor. They attached themselves to one of your arms or legs and squeezed and squeezed until your bones broke. Screw that. Joe wasn't out of the woods yet, though. He still had two attackers, both of whom had to be a good 20 years younger than him. Granted, one was in bad shape, but he still couldn't let down his guard.

In the moments it took for him to knock down KC, Fatty and his buddy had collected themselves off the ground and were coming back at Joe. Branches at the ready to rain down hellfire on Joe. Knocking them both down like bowling pins had served to make them a little more cautious in their approach, but they were still closing in on Joe.

Despite being exhausted, Joe kept light on his feet and moved swiftly to stay out of reach of their improvised weapons. Joe maneuvered himself between Fatty and his club brother so that he only had to deal with one fighter at a time. Fatty took a cumbersome swing at Joe, completely missing him. Joe countered with a hammer fist into Fatty's left temple. Fatty lost his balance and staggered backwards. His buddy side-stepped the stumbling fat guy and raised his branch at Joe. Instead of stepping backwards out of the way, Joe moved in fast, jamming his assailant's right arm back and unleashing a flurry of punches to the man's face as Joe's left arm pinned the man's right arm back.

Tiring from the repeated punches he unleashed on the younger biker, Joe pushed the Dark Legion bro away from him. The guy was stunned but not out. He pulled away from the battered man and swung back to see where the fat guy had gone. His heart was pounding, and he knew he probably only had a minute or more's fight left in him before he would be thoroughly exhausted.

Joe risked looking at the crowd. As far as he could tell, most of the townsfolk still seemed more supportive of him than the Dark Legion guys. Or were they just here purely for the blood lust and didn't care who won as long as they saw some blood? Probably the latter, since most of the townsfolk knew who he was but didn't have a deep connection to him like they would with their friends and close family. In the quick scan of the crowd, he could see the Sheriff standing back behind the crowd, watching unimpressed, with his arms folded. Thanks for nothing, Officer Friendly. If the Sheriff had done his job and intercepted these clowns before they made it to Pine Hollow, none of this would be happening. Still, he had a long-held personal code of never calling the cops. He wasn't going to start begging now.

He turned back to see Fatty struggling to breathe, already gassed out. There was a lot to be said about cardio training. If he got out of this mess intact, he vowed to take up jogging and jumping rope again. Joe's second assailant had given up the tree branch, tossing it aside. Sometimes weapons were more of a hindrance than a help. If you swung on someone with a baseball bat or tree branch and connected, you could do far more damage to your enemy than fists or boots, but if you missed, it would leave you very vulnerable to counterattacks. This guy had finally realized that and was coming at Joe with his left fist raised and his right arm by his side as if they were about to box a few rounds in the gym.

Joe closed the gap with both fists raised. He circled the younger biker and looked for an opening. In return, the younger guy shot a few half assed jabs at Joe's face. Joe easily moved out of the way of them. As he circled around again, he kicked the overweight Dark Legion attacker in the leg. Not just to hurt him but to keep him from doubling up on Joe. Fatty yelped in pain as Joe's engineer boot made contact with the nerves in his leg. Someone in the crowd groaned in mutual support of the Dark Legion fighter.

Joe got a few decent punches to the younger Dark Legion guy as they continued to spar. For an older guy, he really felt he was doing pretty well, holding his own. In fact, it's damn good. He had surprised himself. With his back to the crowd now, he continued to look for holes in his enemies' defenses. Firing off a few more solid punches to the body and face of his opponent, hurting the man.

Just as Joe thought he might actually win this, he was knocked to the ground by a hard blow to the back. In shock, he rolled to the right to see another of the Dark Legion men rolling on the ground, scrambling to get up. He must have done a flying leap onto Joe's back when he was fighting the other guy. Before he had a chance to get up out of the dirt, he received a hard kick to his ribs from the right. The pain was instantaneous. He had probably cracked or broken some ribs. From his peripheral vision, he could see it was another of the Dark Legion who had kicked him when he was down. He was tired, bloodied and beaten, and now he was facing 3 younger fighters. His heart sank; he didn't have much left in him now. This was bad.

CHAPTER 34

Ryder weaved his way through the cluster of parked cars, trying to spot Vince. His mind worked through all the different scenarios of picking him out in the crowd and how to handle that. Stab him in close quarters and slip back through the crowd before anyone had realized what had happened? Drag him away from the crowd and then attack him? What to do? What to do?

As he was running through the various options in his head, he realized that Vince was standing away from the crowd, closer to the parked crowd than the drunken spectators. Of all the luck! It seemed to Ryder that he had his arms folded and was watching the bikers below duke it out. Strange way to do police work, but it was Vince, someone who had always broken the law.

Ever so carefully, Ryder grabbed the Mossberg from his vest pocket and pulled it out. He held it upside down by its grip so his forearm concealed it as he contemplated his next move. He had been living on anger his whole life. Before prison, it was his rotten childhood, no love, no money, nothing. Everyone he had ever known had sold him out. His family, his school, his friends, the justice system. What did he have to lose? Nothing. No. That wasn't true; he had Leanne waiting for him back in Coyote Ridge.

If he shot Vince, would Leanne ever forgive him? Probably not. Still easy for her; his whole life had been taken from him by Vince's treachery. Why did he choose to sell out their friendship for money? Was any amount of money worth that betrayal? He didn't know. Right now, it didn't matter. He had Vince in his sights. He checked his weapon quickly, ensuring it was loaded and the safety off.

'Hey, Hey Vince," he half-whispered to his enemy.

Vince continued to watch the fights. Ryder noted the older man was now on the ground, getting kicked by the other guys. What douche bags. When he was a kid, two boys would fight it out. If one went down, you gave him a chance to get back up to continue the fight. If he didn't get up, the fight was over. You didn't have your friends rat pack the guy. No sportsmanship these days.

"Vinnnnccceeee," he hissed. He readied the Mossberg.

Vince turned around. Ryder could see the man trying to process the situation. Eyeing Ryder's weapon, Vince reached for his.

"Don't," Ryder said softly.

Vince stared back at him.

'Ryder? Is that you?" he asked, almost sobbing.

"Yes," Ryder replied.

Vince went to say something.

Ryder aimed for center mass and squeezed the trigger.

Just for a moment, it felt like all time had stopped. Everything was in slow motion.

Then, a thunder clap from Ryder's Mossberg went off. Vince crying out in pain. Blood flying through the air. The fighting stopped. One of the female spectators near the back stared, her brain trying to process what just happened.

"OH MY GOD HE SHOT THE SHERIFF," she shrieked.

Some of the women in the crowd screamed. Everyone started to run for their cars. Widespread panic.

What surprised Ryder was that no one was coming to Vince's aid. He slowly turned and walked back towards his bike. He shoved the firearm back into his backpack. Despite being parked near the entrance gate, it was now impossible to leave. He would be crushed by all the pickup trucks and cars trying to get the hell out of there.

The fighting had stopped, too. The younger bike club guys were grabbing their bloodied friends and attempting to get out of dodge, too.

Ryder would wait until everyone cleared out and then leave. Would he go see Leanne? If he did, he couldn't lie to her about what he had done. Maybe he should just head right back to California now? He could head East, too, just get on his scooter and ride. That was another option.

As the multiple cars and trucks made their way out of the car park, Ryder, who sat on his Harley, could hear another vehicle somewhere on the main road honking. *Now what?* He thought. Maybe someone had forgotten something in the car park and was turning around to make their way back in? Deep down, he didn't care. He had spent 20 years waiting for this day, and now that he had killed Vince, he felt no better. If anything, he felt empty or even worse, numb.

As he waited for the last of their vehicles to depart, the older biker who had been in the middle of the field fighting the rival club guys approached Ryder with his arms raised, in the "hands up, don't shoot" position.

"Hey, I'm unarmed," Joe said to Ryder.

'So am I," said Ryder.

The older biker looked surprised but didn't say anything.

'I don't know who you are, but you saved my life," said Joe to Ryder.

"I'm Ryder. What's your name?" asked Ryder, extending his hand for Joe to shake.

"I'm Joe. Sorry, can't shake your hand. Something is definitely broken in mine. He held his busted right hand up for Ryder to see. 'Think it's a knuckle or something"

"You going to be okay to ride?" asked Ryder.

Joe moved his remaining fingers. 'It's gonna hurt like a mofo, but I think so"

"Well, let me know if you need any help," Ryder replied.

"Why did you shoot the Sheriff?" asked Joe.

Ryder sighed, "It's a long story."

As they were talking, a lone vehicle pulled into the car park. To Ryder's surprise, it was Leanne.

She parked up and ran towards Ryder. Joe, realizing that the new arrival knew Ryder, said his goodbyes and wandered off. First, he was going to collect his hidden pistol, then start his bike and try to ride home. He needed some ibuprofen and a cold shower to clean himself up. He tried to think if he had any ice packs at home. If not, he would have to create a makeshift one with a plastic shopping bag and ice cubes from the freezer. He had the feeling that he was going to be bruised and busted up for at least the next two weeks.

Leanne reached Ryder and grabbed him in a huge hug. They held each other tight for a moment, and then she pulled away.

"Oh my god. I have been so worried. I thought you might have done something stupid," she exclaimed.

'I shot Vince," said Ryder quietly, almost under his breath.

"Whattttt?" asked Leanne. It was like her brain couldn't process what was happening.

"I SHOT VINCE," said Ryder, this time much louder.

"No, no, no. Tell me you didn't," sobbed Leanne.

"I'm sorry," said Ryder. "I had to"

In a panic, Leanne looked over the now abandoned car park. There, near his patrol car, lay the body of downed Sheriff Williams. She screamed and ran towards the prone law enforcement officer.

Ryder saw this as his signal to leave. That settled it. He would ride to Flagstaff tonight, find a room, stay the night and head back to California in the morning. He felt emotionally and spiritually exhausted. He would deal with whatever legal ramifications were coming for him in the morning.

CHAPTER 35

Pine Hollow, Arizona.

It took Joe a little over 2 weeks to heal up. The cracked ribs were the worst; every time he laughed or coughed, pain racked his whole body. He hadn't bothered going to the doctor for his hand; he just bought some surgical tape and taped the two damaged fingers together. Despite all his injuries, he had only missed a day at the motorcycle shop. Clay and Nina returned from vacation and were very pleased he hadn't burnt the shop down or left town.

Looking back, he was glad he had stood his ground and hadn't tried to run. If he had run, he would have been looking over his shoulder for the rest of his life. He had faced the challenge head-on and had lived to tell the tale. He doubted the Dark Legion guys would be back. If they did, well, he would be waiting for them.

CHAPTER 36

Flagstaff, Arizona.

Ryder awoke to his cell phone ringing. As he tried to clear the fog from his brain, he peered through half-sleepy eyes to see who was calling him so early. It was Leanne. Probably wanting to give him another mouthful of abuse for killing her brother-in-law, he figured. Did he really want that? Now? Or any time? He wasn't in the mood for an ear-blasting, but something told him to pick up anyway.

"Hello," he said blearily.

"Hey, it's me. Where are you?" asked Leanne.

"I'm in Flagstaff. Why?" Ryder asked.

"I'm in Flagstaff too," Leanne said.

What on earth was she doing in Flag? Did she work with law enforcement to hunt me down?

"What are you doing in Flagstaff?" he asked.

"I'm at the Flagstaff Medical Center," Leanne explained 'Can you come meet me?"

"Everything okay?" asked Ryder.

"Just get here. 1200 North Beaver Street. Top Floor," said Leanne, "Have to go, Bye."

Just like that, she hung up on him.

Well, I guess I'm going to the hospital, Ryder shrugged, *like I have a say in the matter.*

He quickly got dressed, checked out of his motel room and rode over to the medical center. He took the elevator to the top and gave Leanne's name. The duty nurse seemed unfazed and sent him down the hall. Just as he was about to enter the room, Leanne came out, nearly walking right into him.

"Leanne, you okay?" he asked.

"I'm fine," she replied 'It's Vince."

It took a moment for Ryder to figure out what she meant. *Vince was alive and in that hospital room? How was that possible?*

"Vince is alive?" he asked.

"Yes! He's alive and he wants to see you."

"Oh fuck that. I'm not going in there," Ryder replied.

"It's okay. Just go in. He's expecting you," said Leanne softly.

"You don't get it. I can't," said Ryder.

"Babe, just go in. It's gonna be okay," Leanne reassured Ryder.

Every fiber of Ryder's being was screaming at him to turn and run, but something made him stay. Leanne took his hand and led him to the door to Vince's room.

"Go on, you big baby," she chided, pushing him through the door against his better judgment.

Ryder entered the room. Sure enough, there was Vince. Propped up on his hospital bed, his left arm heavily bandaged and him wired up to a bunch of serious-looking medical machines.

'Ryder?" asked Vince in a quiet voice.

"Hey," said Ryder, ready to turn and run out the door at any second.

'I'm sorry, man. I'm so sorry," said Vince, "I fucked up big time."

Ryder realized he should be asking how Vince was doing. Would he be okay? How did he survive? Questions like that. But, he couldn't help himself.

'Why, bro? Why?" he asked.

"I got in bad with some heavy people. If I didn't pay them what I owed them, they were going to kill my family," Vince explained.

'Oh,' was all Ryder could say to that.

'There's not a day that has gone by that I haven't regretted my decision," said Vince. "I knew you would come for me, and rightfully so. You never sell your friends out," He was crying now.

"No, you don't," said Ryder.

'I know there is nothing I can ever do to make it better," Vince continued, "But for what it's worth, I really am sorry."

"Okay," said Ryder.

"Also, don't worry. I told the cops it was one of the Dark Legion guys who shot me," said Vince.

"Oh," said Ryder. *So that's who those guys were. The Dark Legion.*

"Brother. Again, I am so sorry for everything I did to you. I was young and dumb. Not thinking right," said Vince, lying in agony in his bed.

Ryder didn't know what to say. So, he just stood there staring at Vince.

Ryder no longer knew what he felt now. Or what to do. He had spent 20 years plotting revenge against Vince. He had got it. Why did he feel so numb? He didn't know what to say next to Vince.

'Hey, I gotta go," said Ryder. "Get well soon," was all he could manage before turning and walking out the door.

As soon as he exited, Leanne collared him.

'Well?" she asked.

"He's alive," said Ryder

"Yeah. His bulletproof vest took the majority of the blast, but some fragments went into his arm. He's expected to make a full recovery," Leanne explained excitedly.

"Okay, that's good, I guess," said Ryder. 'Hey, I gotta go"

'What? You're leaving?" asked Leanne.

'Yeah, I gotta go," said Ryder, "I'll call you in a day or so."

'Are you kidding me?" she asked, barely able to control her anger.

"I gotta go," was all he could manage to say. 'Sorry"

"No, Ryder, please stay," sobbed Leanne, fighting back tears.

"I'll call you. I promise," said Ryder, walking back towards the elevator bank.

He left the hospital and started up his bike, heading back towards California. Ryder reflected on the last few weeks. It had been a bittersweet time. Unsure of his destination and haunted by his decisions. He had left behind a legacy of betrayal, love and hard-won redemption.

Thank You!

Hey this is Alex. If you have made it this far, Thank you!

I had a lot of fun writing this novel and I wanted to thank you for reading it.

If you enjoyed Deserted Loyalty – An Outlaw Biker Tale please consider leaving a review on Amazon as that would greatly help me out.

Please also check out my novel : Broken Brotherhood – An Outlaw Biker Tale

https://www.amazon.com/Broken-Brotherhood-Outlaw-Biker-Tale-ebook/dp/B0F2LMNBHD

I've a ton of stories in the pipeline if you want to keep updated on new books head on over to my website : www.alexmcrae.net.

Also feel free to follow me on Amazon here:
https://www.amazon.com/stores/Alex-McRae/author/B0F344WTHB

All for now

Alex

Arizona 2025

Extra special thanks to the following people:

Mooch, The Motorcycle Prophet, George Christie Jr, James 2, Hugo Dias and Jeremy Rogers.

www.ingramcontent.com/pod-product-compliance
Lightning Source LLC
Chambersburg PA
CBHW032132170626
46808CB00006B/2201